The

S. W. F. CLUB

By

CAROLINE E. JACOBS

Author of

"JOAN'S JOLLY VACATION"
"JOAN OF JUNIPER INN"
"PATRICIA," ETC.

THE GOLDSMITH PUBLISHING CO.
CHICAGO

CONTENTS

CHAPTER I
PAULINE'S FLAG

THE S. W. F. CLUB

CHAPTER I

PAULINE'S FLAG

PAULINE dropped the napkin she was hemming and, leaning back in her chair, stared soberly down into the rain-swept garden.

Overhead, Patience was having a "clarin' up scrape" in her particular corner of the big garret, to the tune of "There's a Good Time Coming."

Pauline drew a quick breath; probably, there was a good time coming—any number of them —only they were not coming her way; they would go right by on the main road, they always did.

" 'There's a good time coming,' " Patience insisted shrilly, " 'Help it on! Help it on!' "

Pauline drew another quick breath. She would help them on! If they would none of them stop on their own account, they must be flagged. And—yes, she would do it—right now.

Getting up, she brought her writing-portfolio from the closet, clearing a place for it on the little table before the window. Then her eyes went back to the dreary, rain-soaked garden. How did one begin a letter to an uncle one had never seen; and of whom one meant to ask a great favor?

But at last, after more than one false start, the letter got itself written, after a fashion.

Pauline read it over to herself, a little dissatisfied pucker between her brows:—

Mr. Paul Almy Shaw,
    New York City, New York.

MY DEAR UNCLE PAUL: First, I should like you to understand that neither father nor mother know that I am writing this letter to you; and that if they did, I think they would forbid it; and I should like you to believe, too, that if it were not for Hilary I should not dream of writing it. You know so little about us, that perhaps you do not remember which of us Hilary is. She comes next to me, and is just thirteen. She hasn't been well for a long time, not since she had to leave school last winter, and the doctor says that what she needs is a thorough change. Mother and I have talked it over and over, but we simply can't manage it. I would try to earn some money, but I haven't a single accomplishment; besides I don't see how I could leave home, and anyway it would take so long, and Hilary needs a change now. And so I am writing to ask you to please help us out a little. I do hope you won't be angry at my asking; and I hope very, very much, that you will answer favorably.

I remain,

Very respectfully,

Pauline Almy Shaw.

Winton, Vt., May Sixteenth.

Pauline laughed rather nervously as she slipped her letter into an envelope and addressed it. It wasn't a very big flag, but perhaps it would serve her purpose.

Tucking the letter into her blouse, Pauline ran down-stairs to the sitting-room, where her mother and Hilary were. "I'm going down to the post-office, mother," she said; "any errands?"

"My dear, in this rain?"

"There won't be any mail for us, Paul," Hilary said, glancing listlessly up from the book she was trying to read; "you'll only get all wet and uncomfortable for nothing."

Pauline's gray eyes were dancing; "No," she agreed, "I don't suppose there will be any mail for us—to-day; but I want a walk. It won't hurt me, mother. I love to be out in the rain."

And all the way down the slippery village street the girl's eyes continued to dance with excitement. It was so much to have actually started her ball rolling; and, at the moment, it seemed that Uncle Paul must send it bounding back in the promptest and most delightful of letters. He had never married, and somewhere down at the bottom of his apparently crusty, old heart he must have kept a soft spot for the children of his only brother.

Thus Pauline's imagination ran on, until near the post-office she met her father. The whole family had just finished a tour of the West in Mr. Paul Shaw's private car—of course, he must have a private car, wasn't he a big railroad man?—and Pauline had come back to Winton long enough to gather up her skirts a little more firmly when she saw Mr. Shaw struggling up the hill against the wind.

"Pauline!" he stopped, straightening his tall, scholarly figure. "What brought you out in such a storm?"

With a sudden feeling of uneasiness, Pauline wondered what he would say if she were to explain exactly what it was that had brought her out. With an impulse towards at least a half-confession, she said hurriedly, "I wanted to post a letter I'd just written; I'll be home almost as soon as you are, father."

Then she ran on down the street. All at once she felt her courage weakening; unless she got her letter posted immediately she felt she should end by tearing it up.

When it had slipped from her sight through the narrow slit labeled "LETTERS," she stood a moment, almost wishing it were possible to get it back again.

She went home rather slowly. Should she confess at once, or wait until Uncle Paul's answer came? It should be here inside of a week, surely; and if it were favorable—and, oh, it must be favorable—would not that in itself seem to justify her in what she had done?

On the front piazza, Patience was waiting for her, a look of mischief in her blue eyes. Patience was ten, a red-haired, freckled slip of a girl. She danced about Pauline now. "Why didn't you tell me you were going out so I could've gone, too? And what have you been up to, Paul Shaw? Something! You needn't tell me you haven't."

"I'm not going to tell you anything," Pauline answered, going on into the house. The study door was half open, and when she had taken off her things, Pauline stood a moment a little uncertainly outside it. Then suddenly, much to her small sister's disgust, she went in, closing the door behind her.

Mr. Shaw was leaning back in his big chair at one corner of the fireplace. "Well," he asked, looking up, "did you get your letter in in time, my dear?"

"Oh, it wasn't the time." Pauline sat down on a low bench at the other end of the fireplace. "It was that I wanted to feel that it was really mailed. Did you ever feel that way about a letter, father? And as if, if you didn't hurry and get it in—you wouldn't— mail it?"

Something in her tone made her father glance at her more closely; it was very like the tone in which Patience was apt to make her rather numerous confessions. Then it occurred to him, that, whether by accident or design, she was sitting on the very stool on which Patience usually placed herself at such times, and which had gained thereby the name of "the stool of penitence."

"Yes," he answered, "I have written such letters once or twice in my life."

Pauline stooped to straighten out the hearth rug. "Father," she said abruptly; "I have been writing to Uncle Paul." She drew a sharp breath of relief.

"You have been writing to your Uncle Paul! About what, Pauline?"

And Pauline told him. When she had finished, Mr. Shaw sat for some moments without speaking, his eyes on the fire.

"It didn't seem very—wrong, at the time,"

Pauline ventured. "I had to do something for Hilary."

"Why did you not consult your mother, or myself, before taking such a step, Pauline?"

"I was afraid—if I did—that you would—forbid it; and I was so anxious to do something. It's nearly a month now since Dr. Brice said Hilary must have a change. We used to have such good times together—Hilary and I—but we never have fun anymore—she doesn't care about anything; and to-day it seemed as if I couldn't bear it any longer, so I wrote. I—I am sorry, if you're displeased with me, father, and yet, if Uncle Paul writes back favorably, I'm afraid I can't help being glad I wrote."

Mr. Shaw rose, lighting the low reading-lamp, standing on the study table. "You are frank enough after the event, at least, Pauline. To be equally so, I am displeased; displeased and exceedingly annoyed. However, we will let the matter rest where it is until you have heard from your uncle. I should advise your saying nothing to your sisters until his reply comes. I am afraid you will find it disappointing."

Pauline flushed. "I never intended telling Hilary anything about it unless I had good news for her; as for Patience—"

Out in the hall again, with the study door closed behind her, Pauline stood a moment choking back a sudden lump in her throat. Would Uncle Paul treat her letter as a mere piece of school-girl impertinence, as father seemed to?

From the sitting-room came an impatient summons. "Paul, will you never come!"

"What is it, Hilary?" Pauline asked, coming to sit at one end of the old sofa.

"That's what I want to know," Hilary answered from the other end. "Impatience says you've been writing all sorts of mysterious letters this afternoon, and that you came home just now looking like—"

"Well, like what?"

"Like you'd been up to something—and weren't quite sure how the grown-ups were going to take it," Patience explained from the rug before the fire.

"How do you know I have been writing—anything?" Pauline asked.

"There, you see!" Patience turned to Hilary, "she doesn't deny it!"

"I'm not taking the trouble to deny or confirm little girl nonsense," Pauline declared. "But what makes you think I've been writing letters?"

"Oh, 'by the pricking of my thumbs'!" Patience rolled over, and resting her sharp little chin in her hands, stared up at her sisters from under her mop of short red curls. "Pen! Ink! Paper! And such a lot of torn-up scraps! It's really very simple!"

But Pauline was on her way to the dining-room. "Terribly convincing, isn't it?" Her tone should have squelched Patience, but it didn't.

"You can't fool me!" that young person retorted. "I know you've been up to something! And I'm pretty sure father doesn't approve, from the way you waited out there in the hall just now."

Pauline did not answer; she was busy laying the cloth for supper. "Anything up,

Paul?" Hilary urged, following her sister out to the dining-room.

"The barometer—a very little; I shouldn't wonder if we had a clear day to-morrow."

"You are as provoking as Impatience! But I needn't have asked; nothing worth while ever does happen to us."

"You know perfectly well, Pauline Almy Shaw!" Patience proclaimed, from the curtained archway between the rooms. "You know perfectly well, that the ev'dence against you is most in-crim-i-na-ting!" Patience delighted in big words.

"Hilary," Pauline broke in, "I forgot to tell you, I met Mrs. Dane this morning; she wants us to get up a social—'If the young ladies at the parsonage will,' and so forth."

"I hate socials! Besides, there aren't any 'young ladies' at the parsonage; or, at any rate, only one. I shan't have to be a young lady for two years yet."

"Most in-crim-i-na-ting!" Patience repeated insistently; "you wrote."

Pauline turned abruptly and going into the pantry began taking down the cups and saucers for the table. As soon as Hilary had gone back to the sitting-room, she called softly, "Patty, O Patty!"

Patience grinned wickedly; she was seldom called Patty, least of all by Pauline. "Well?" she answered.

"Come here—please," and when Patience was safely inside the pantry, Pauline shut the door gently—"Now see here, Impatience—"

"That isn't what you called me just now!"

"Patty then—Listen, suppose—suppose I have been—trying to do something to—to help Hilary to get well; can't you see that I wouldn't want her to know, until I was sure, really sure, it was going to come to something?"

Patience gave a little jump of excitement. "How jolly! But who have you been writing to—about it, Paul!"

"I haven't said that—"

"See here, Paul, I'll play fair, if you do; but if you go trying to act any 'grown-up sister' business I'll—"

And Pauline capitulated. "I can't tell you about it yet, Patty; father said not to. I want you to promise not to ask questions, or say anything about it, before Hilary. We don't want her to get all worked up, thinking something nice is going to happen, and then maybe have her disappointed."

"Will it be nice—very nice?"

"I hope so."

"And will I be in it?"

"I don't know. I don't know what it'll be, or when it'll be."

"Oh, dear! I wish you did. I can't think who it is you wrote to, Paul. And why didn't father like your doing it?"

"I haven't said that he—"

"Paul, you're very tiresome. Didn't he know you were going to do it?"

Pauline gathered up her cups and saucers without answering.

"Then he didn't." Patience observed. "Does mother know about it?"

"I mean to tell her as soon as I get a good chance," Pauline said impatiently, going back to the dining-room.

When she returned a few moments later, she found Patience still in the pantry, sitting

thoughtfully on the old, blue sugar bucket.
"I know," Patience announced triumphantly.
"You've been writing to Uncle Paul!"

Pauline gasped and fled to the kitchen;
there were times when flight was the better
part of discretion, in dealing with the youngest
member of the Shaw family.

On the whole, Patience behaved very well
that evening, only, on going to bid her father
good-night, did she ask anxiously, how long
it took to send a letter to New York and get
an answer.

"That depends considerably upon the
promptness with which the party written to
answers the letter," Mr. Shaw told her.

"A week?" Patience questioned.

"Probably—if not longer."

Patience sighed.

"Have *you* been writing a letter to someone in New York?" her father asked.

"No, indeed," the child said gravely,
"but," she looked up, answering his glance.
"Paul didn't tell me, father; I—guessed.
Uncle Paul does live in New York, doesn't
he?"

"Yes," Mr. Shaw answered, almost sharply. "Now run to bed, my dear."

But when the stairs were reached, Patience most certainly did not run. "I think people are very queer," she said to herself, "they seem to think *ten* years isn't a bit more grown-up than six or seven."

"Mummy," she asked, when later her mother came to take away her light, "father and Uncle Paul are brethren, aren't they?"

"My dear! What put that into your head?"

"Aren't they?"

"Certainly, dear."

"Then why don't they 'dwell together in unity'?"

"Patience!" Mrs. Shaw stared down at the sharp inquisitive little face.

"Why don't they?" Patience persisted. If persistency be a virtue, Patience was to be highly commended.

"My dear, who has said that they do not?"

Patience shrugged; as if things had always to be said. "But, mummy—"

"Go to sleep now, dear." Mrs. Shaw bent to kiss her good-night.

"All the same," Patience confided to the darkness, "I know they don't." She gave a little shiver of delight—something very mysterious was afoot evidently.

Out on the landing, Mrs. Shaw found Pauline waiting for her. "Come into your room, mother, please, I've started up the fire; I want to tell you something."

"I thought as much," her mother answered. She sat down in the big armchair and Pauline drew up before the fire. "I've been expecting it all the evening."

Pauline dropped down on the floor, her head against her mother's knee. "This family is dreadfully keen-sighted. Mother dear, please don't be angry—" and Pauline made confession.

When she had finished, Mrs. Shaw sat for some moments, as her husband had done, her eyes on the fire. "You told him that we could not manage it, Pauline?" she said at last. "My dear, how could you!"

"But, mother dear, I was—desperate; something has to be done for—Hilary, and I had to do it!"

"Do you suppose your father and I do not realize that quite as well as you do, Pauline?"

"You and I have talked it over and over, and father never says—anything."

"Not to you, perhaps; but he is giving the matter very careful consideration, and later he hopes—"

"Mother dear, that is so indefinite!" Pauline broke in. "And I can't see—Father is Uncle Paul's only brother! If I were rich, and Hilary were not and needed things, I would want her to let me know."

"It is possible, that under certain conditions, Hilary would not wish you to know." Mrs. Shaw hesitated, then she said slowly, "You know, Pauline, that your uncle is much older than your father; so much older, that he seemed to stand—when your father was a boy—more in the light of a father to him, than an older brother. He was much opposed to your father's going into the ministry, he wanted him to go into business with him. He is a strong-willed man, and does not easily relinquish any plan of his own making. It went hard with him, when your father refused to yield; later,

when your father received the call to this
parish, your uncle quite as strongly opposed
his accepting it—burying himself alive in a
little out-of-the-way hole, he called it. It
came to the point, finally, on your uncle's in-
sisting on his making it a choice between himself and Winton. He refused to ever come
near the place and the two or three letters
your father wrote at first remained unan-
swered. The breach between them has been
one of the hardest trials your father has had
to bear."

"Oh," Pauline cried miserably, "what a hor-
rid interfering thing father must think me!
Rushing in where I had no right to! I wish
I'd known—I just thought—you see, father
speaks of Uncle Paul now and then—that maybe they'd only—grown apart—and that if
Uncle Paul knew! But perhaps my letter
will get lost. It would serve me right; and
yet, if it does, I'm afraid I can't help feeling somewhat disappointed—on Hilary's account."

Her mother smiled. "We can only wait
and see. I would rather you said nothing of

what I have been telling you to either Hilary
or Patience, Pauline."

"I won't, Mother Shaw. It seems I have a
lot of secrets from Hilary. And I won't write
any more such letters without consulting you
or father, you can depend on that."

Mr. Paul Shaw's answer did not come within the allotted week. It was the longest week
Pauline had ever known; and when the second
went by and still no word from her uncle, the
waiting and uncertainty became very hard to
bear, all the harder, that her usual confidant,
Hilary, must not be allowed to suspect anything.

The weather had turned suddenly warm, and
Hilary's listlessness had increased proportion-
ately, which probably accounted for the dying
out of what little interest she had felt at first
in Patience's "mysterious letter."

Patience, herself, was doing her best to play
fair; fortunately, she was in school the greater
part of the day, else the strain upon her powers of self-control might have proved too
heavy.

"Mother," Pauline said one evening, lingering in her mother's room, after Hilary had gone to bed, "I don't believe Uncle Paul means answering at all. I wish I'd never asked him to do anything."

"So do I, Pauline. Still it is rather early yet for you to give up hope. It's hard waiting, I know, dear, but that is something we all have to learn to do, sooner or later."

"I don't think 'no news is good news,'" Pauline said; then she brightened. "Oh, Mother Shaw! Suppose the letter is on the way now, and that Hilary is to have a sea voyage! *You'd* have to go, too."

"Pauline, Pauline, not so fast! Listen, dear, we might send Hilary out to The Maples for a week or two. Mrs. Boyd would be delighted to have her; and it wouldn't be too far away, in case we should be getting her ready for that—sea voyage."

"I don't believe she'd care to go; it's quieter than here at home."

"But it would be a change. I believe I'll suggest it to her in the morning."

But when Mrs. Shaw did suggest it the next morning, Hilary was quite of Pauline's opinion. "I shouldn't like it a bit, mother! It would be worse than home—duller, I mean; and Mrs. Boyd would fuss over me so," she said impatiently.

"You used to like going there, Hilary."

"Mother, you can't want me to go."

"I think it might do you good, Hilary. I should like you to try it."

"Please, mother, I don't see the use of bothering with little half-way things."

"I do, Hilary, when they are the only ones within reach."

The girl moved restlessly, settling her hammock cushions; then she lay looking out over the sunny garden with discontented eyes.

It was a large old-fashioned garden, separated on the further side by a low hedge from the old ivy-covered church. On the back steps of the church, Sextoness Jane was shaking out her duster. She was old and gray and insignificant looking; her duties as sexton, in which she had succeeded her father, were her great delight. The will with which she sang and worked now seemed to have in it something of reproach for the girl stretched out idly in the hammock. Nothing more than half-way things, and not too many of those, had ever come Sextoness Jane's way. Yet she was singing now over her work.

Hilary moved impatiently, turning her back on the garden and the bent old figure moving about in the church beyond; but, somehow, she couldn't turn her back on what that bent old figure had suddenly come to stand for.

Fifteen minutes later, she sat up, pushing herself slowly back and forth. "I wish Jane had chosen any other morning to clean the church in, Mother Shaw!" she protested with spirit.

Her mother looked up from her mending. "Why, dear? It is her regular day."

"Couldn't she do it, I wonder, on an irregular day! Anyhow, if she had, I shouldn't have to go to The Maples this afternoon. Must I take a trunk, mother?"

"Hilary! But what has Jane to do with your going?"

"Pretty nearly everything, I reckon. Must I, mother?"

"No, indeed, dear; and you are not to go at all, unless you can do it willingly."

"Oh, I'm fairly resigned; don't press me too hard, Mother Shaw. I think I'll go tell Paul now."

"Well," Pauline said, "I'm glad you've decided to go, Hilary. I—that is, maybe it won't be for very long."

CHAPTER II
THE MAPLES

CHAPTER II

THE MAPLES

THAT afternoon Pauline drove Hilary out to the big, busy, pleasant farm, called The Maples.

As they jogged slowly down the one principal street of the sleepy, old town, Pauline tried to imagine that presently they would turn off down the by-road, leading to the station. Through the still air came the sound of the afternoon train, panting and puffing to be off with as much importance as the big train, which later, it would connect with down at the junction.

"Paul," Hilary asked suddenly, "what are you thinking about?"

Pauline slapped the reins lightly across old Fanny's plump sides. "Oh, different things— traveling for one." Suppose Uncle Paul's letter should come in this afternoon's mail!

That she would find it waiting for her when she got home!

"So was I," Hilary said. "I was wishing that you and I were going off on that train, Paul."

"Where to?" Paul asked. After all, it couldn't do any harm—Hilary would think it one of their "pretend" talks, and it would be nice to have some definite basis to build on later.

"Anywhere," Hilary answered. "I would like to go to the seashore somewhere; but most anywhere, where there were people and interesting things to do and see, would do."

"Yes," Pauline agreed.

"There's Josie," Hilary said, and her sister drew rein, as a girl came to the edge of the walk to speak to them.

"Going away?" she asked, catching sight of the valise.

"Only out to the Boyds'," Pauline told her, "to leave Hilary."

Josie shifted the strap of school-books under her arm impatiently. " 'Only!' " she repeated. "Well, I just wish I was going, too;

it's a deal pleasanter out there, than in a stuffy school room these days."

"It's stupid—and you both know it," Hilary protested. She glanced enviously at Josie's strap of books. "And when school closes, you'll be through for good, Josie Brice. We shan't finish together, after all, now."

"Oh, I'm not through yet," Josie assured her. "Father'll be going out past The Maples Saturday morning, I'll get him to take me along."

Hilary brightened. "Don't forget," she urged, and as she and Pauline drove on, she added, "I suppose I can stick it out for a week."

"Well, I should think as much. *Will* you go on, Fanny!" Pauline slapped the dignified, complacent Fanny with rather more severity than before. "She's one great mass of laziness," she declared. "Father's spoiled her a great deal more than he ever has any of us."

It was a three-mile drive from the village to The Maples, through pleasant winding roads, hardly deserving of a more important title than lane. Now and then, from the top of a low hill, they caught a glimpse of the great lake beyond, shining in the afternoon sunlight, a little ruffled by the light breeze sweeping down to it from the mountains bordering it on the further side.

Hilary leaned back in the wide shaded gig; she looked tired, and yet the new touch of color in her cheeks was not altogether due to weariness. "The ride's done you good," Pauline said.

"I wonder what there'll be for supper," Hilary remarked. "You'll stay, Paul?"

"If you promise to eat a good one." It was comforting to have Hilary actually wondering what they would have.

They had reached the broad avenue of maples leading from the road up to the house. It was a long, low, weather-stained house, breathing an unmistakable air of generous and warm-hearted hospitality. Pauline never came to it, without a sense of pity for the kindly elderly couple, who were so fond of young folks, and who had none of their own.

Mrs. Boyd had seen them coming, and she came out to meet them, as they turned into the dooryard. And an old dog, sunning himself on the doorstep, rose with a slow wag of welcome.

"Mother's sent you something she was sure you would like to have," Pauline said. "Please, will you take in a visitor for a few days?" she added, laying a hand on Hilary's.

"You've brought Hilary out to stop?" Mrs. Boyd cried delightedly. "Now I call that mighty good of your mother. You come right 'long in, both of you: you're sure you can't stop, too, Pauline?"

"Only to supper, thank you."

Mrs. Boyd had the big valise out from under the seat by now. "Come right 'long in," she repeated. "You're tired, aren't you, Hilary? But a good night's rest'll set you up wonderful. Take her into the spare room, Pauline. Dear me, I must have felt you was coming, seeing that I aired it out beautiful only this morning. I'll go call Mr. Boyd to take Fanny to the barn."

"Isn't she the dearest thing!" Pauline declared, as she and Hilary went indoors.

The spare room was back of the parlor, a

large comfortable room, with broad windows facing south and west, and a small vine-covered porch all it's own on the south side of the room.

Pauline pulled forward a great chintz-cushioned rocker, putting her sister into it, and opened the porch door. Beyond lay a wide, sloping meadow and beyond the meadow, the lake sparkled and rippled in the sunshine.

"If you're not contented here, Hilary Shaw!" Pauline said, standing in the low door-way. "Suppose you pretend you've never been here before! I reckon you'd travel a long ways to find a nicer place to stay in."

"I shouldn't doubt it if you were going to stay with me, Paul; I know I'm going to be homesick."

Pauline stretched out a hand to Captain, the old dog, who had come around to pay his compliments. Captain liked visitors—when he was convinced that they really were visitors, not peddlers, nor agents, quite as well as his master and mistress did. "You'd be home-sick enough, if you really were off on your travels—you'd better get used to it. Hadn't she, Captain?" Pauline went to unpack the valise, opening the drawers of the old-fashioned mahogany bureau with a little breath of pleasure. "Lavender! Hilary."

Hilary smiled, catching some of her sister's enthusiasm. She leaned back among her cushions, her eyes on the stretch of shining water at the far end of the pasture. "I wish you were going to be here, Paul, so that we could go rowing. I wonder if I'll ever feel as if I could row again, myself."

"Of course you will, and a great deal sooner than you think." Pauline hung Hilary's dressing-gown across the foot of the high double bed. "Now I think you're all settled, ma'am, and I hope to your satisfaction. Isn't it a veritable 'chamber of peace,' Hilary?"

Through the open door and windows came the distant tinkle of a cow bell, and other farm sounds. There came, too, the scent of the early May pinks growing in the borders of Mrs. Boyd's old-fashioned flower beds. Already the peace and quiet of the house, the homely comfort, had done Hilary good; the thought of the long simple days to come, were not so depressing as they had seemed when thought of that morning.

"Bless me, I'd forgotten, but I've a bit of news for you," Mrs. Boyd said, coming in, a moment or so later; "the manor's taken for the summer."

"Really?" Pauline cried, "why it's been empty for ever and ever so long."

The manor was an old rambling stone house, standing a little back from a bit of sandy beach, that jutted out into the lake about a mile from The Maples. It was a pleasant place, with a tiny grove of its own, and good-sized garden, which, year after year, in spite of neglect, was bright with old-fashioned hardy annuals planted long ago, when the manor had been something more than an old neglected house, at the mercy of a chance tenant.

"Just a father and daughter. They've got old Betsy Todd to look after them," Mrs. Boyd went on. "The girl's about your age, Hilary. You wasn't looking to find company of that sort so near, was you?"

Hilary looked interested. "No," she answered. "But, after all, the manor's a mile away."

"Oh, she's back and forth every day—for milk, or one thing or another; she's terribly interested in the farm; father's taken a great notion to her. She'll be over after supper, you'll see; and then I'll make you acquainted with her."

"Are they city people?" Pauline asked.

"From New York!" Mrs. Boyd told her proudly. From her air one would have supposed she had planned the whole affair expressly for Hilary's benefit. "Their name's Dayre."

"What is the girl's first name?" Pauline questioned.

"Shirley; it's a queer name for a girl, to my thinking."

"Is she pretty?" Pauline went on.

"Not according to my notions; father says she is. She's thin and dark, and I never did see such a mane of hair—and it ain't always too tidy, neither—but she has got nice eyes and a nice friendly way of talking. Looks to me, like she hasn't been brought up by a woman."

"She sounds—interesting," Pauline said, and when Mrs. Boyd had left them, to make a few changes in her supper arrangements, Pauline turned eagerly to Hilary. "You're in luck, Hilary Shaw! The newest kind of new people; even if it isn't a new place!"

"How do you know they'll, or rather, she'll, want to know me?" Hilary asked, with one of those sudden changes of mood an invalid often shows, "or I her? We haven't seen her yet. Paul, do you suppose Mrs. Boyd would mind letting me have supper in here?"

"Oh, Hilary, she's laid the table in the living-room! I heard her doing it. She'd be ever so disappointed."

"Well," Hilary said, "come on then."

Out in the living-room, they found Mr. Boyd waiting for them, and so heartily glad to see them, that Hilary's momentary impatience vanished. To Pauline's delight, she really brought quite an appetite to her supper.

"You should've come out here long ago, Hilary," Mr. Boyd told her, and he insisted on her having a second helping of the creamed toast, prepared especially in her honor.

Before supper was over, Captain's deep-toned bark proclaimed a newcomer, or new-comers, seeing that it was answered immediately by a medley of shrill barks, in the midst of which a girl's voice sounded authoritively —"Quiet, Phil! Pat, I'm ashamed of you! Pudgey, if you're not good instantly, you shall stay at home to-morrow night!"

A moment later, the owner of the voice appeared at the porch door. "May I come in, Mrs. Boyd?" she asked.

"Come right in, Miss Shirley. I've a couple of young friends here, I want you should get acquainted with," Mrs. Boyd cried.

"You ain't had your supper yet, have you, Miss Shirley?" Mr. Boyd asked.

"Father and I had tea out on the lake," Shirley answered, "but I'm hungry enough again by now, for a slice of Mrs. Boyd's bread and butter."

And presently, she was seated at the table, chatting away with Paul and Hilary, as if they were old acquaintances, asking Mr. Boyd various questions about farm matters and answering Mrs. Boyd's questions regarding

Betsy Todd and her doings, with the most delightful air of good comradeship imaginable.

"Oh, me!" Pauline pushed back her chair regretfully, "I simply must go, it'll be dark before I get home, as it is."

"I reckon it will, deary," Mrs. Boyd agreed, "so I won't urge you to stay longer. Father, you just whistle to Colin to bring Fanny 'round."

Hilary followed her sister into the bedroom. "You'll be over soon, Paul?"

Pauline, putting on her hat before the glass, turned quickly. "As soon as I can. Hilary, don't you like her?"

Hilary balanced herself on the arm of the big, old-fashioned rocker. "I think so. Anyway, I love to watch her talk; she talks all over her face."

They went out to the gig, where Mr. and Mrs. Boyd and Shirley were standing. Shirley was feeding Fanny with handfuls of fresh grass. "Isn't she a fat old dear!" she said.

"She's a fat old poke!" Pauline returned.

"Mayn't I give you a lift? I can go 'round by the manor road 's well as not."

Shirley accepted readily, settling herself in the gig, and balancing her pail of milk on her knee carefully.

"Good-by," Pauline called. "Mind, you're to be ever and ever so much better, next time I come, Hilary."

"Your sister has been sick?" Shirley asked, her voice full of sympathetic interest.

"Not sick—exactly; just run down and list-less."

Shirley leaned a little forward, drawing in long breaths of the clear evening air. "I don't see how anyone can ever get run down—here, in this air; I'm hardly indoors at all. Father and I have our meals out on the porch. You ought to have seen Betsy Todd's face, the first time I proposed it. 'Ain't the dining-room to your liking, miss?'" she asked.

"Betsy Todd's a queer old thing," Pauline commented. "Father has the worst time, get-ting her to come to church."

"We were there last Sunday," Shirley said. "I'm afraid we were rather late; it's a pretty

old church, isn't it?   I suppose you live in that
square white house next to it?"

"Yes," Pauline answered.   "Father came
to Winton just after he was married, so we
girls have never lived anywhere else nor been
anywhere else—that counted.   Any really big
city, I mean.   We're dreadfully tired of Winton—Hilary, especially."

"It's a mighty pretty place."

"I   suppose   so."   Pauline   slapped   old
Fanny impatiently.   "Will you go on!"

Fanny was making forward most reluctantly; the Boyd barn had been very much
to her liking.   Now, as the three dogs made
a swift rush at her leaping and barking around
her, she gave a snort of disgust, quickening her
pace involuntarily.

"Don't call them off, please!" Pauline
begged Shirley.   "She isn't in the least scared,
and it's perfectly refreshing to find that she
can move."

"All the same, discipline must be main-
tained," Shirley insisted; and at her command
the dogs fell behind.

"Have you been here long?" Pauline asked.

"About two weeks. We were going further up the lake—just on a sketching trip,—and we saw this house from the deck of the boat; it looked so delightful, and so deserted and lonely, that we came back from the next landing to see about it. We took it at once and sent for a lot of traps from the studio at home, they aren't here yet."

Pauline looked her interest. It seemed a very odd, attractive way of doing things, no long tiresome plannings of ways and means beforehand. Suppose—when Uncle Paul's letter came—they could set off in such fashion, with no definite point in view, and stop wherever they felt like it.

"I can't think," Shirley went on, "'how such a charming old place came to be standing idle."

"Isn't it rather—run down?"

"Not enough to matter—really. I want father to buy it, and do what is needed to it, without making it all new and snug looking. The sunsets from that front lawn are gorgeous, don't you think so?"

"Yes," Pauline agreed, "I haven't been

over there in two years. We used to have
picnics near there."

"I hope you will again, this summer, and
invite father and me. We adore picnics;
we've had several since we came—he and I and
the dogs. The dogs do love picnics so, too."

Pauline had given up wanting to hurry
Fanny; what a lot she would have to tell her
mother when she got home.

She was sorry when a turn in the road
brought them within sight of the old manor
house. "There's father!" Shirley said, nodding to a figure coming towards them across
a field. The dogs were off to meet him directly, with shrill barks of pleasure.

"May I get down here, please?" Shirley
asked. "Thank you very much for the lift;
and I am so glad to have met you and your
sister, Miss Shaw. You'll both come and see
me soon, won't you?"

"We'd love to," Pauline answered heartily;
" 'cross lots, it's not so very far over here from
the parsonage, and," she hesitated, "you—
you'll be seeing Hilary quite often, while she's
at The Maples, perhaps?"

"I hope so. Father's on the lookout for a horse and rig for me, and then she and I can have some drives together. She will know where to find the prettiest roads."

"Oh, she would enjoy that," Pauline said eagerly, and as she drove on, she turned more than once to glance back at the tall, slender figure crossing the field. Shirley seemed to walk as if the mere act of walking were in itself a pleasure. Pauline thought she had never before known anyone who appeared so alive from head to foot.

"Go 'long, Fanny!" she commanded; she was in a hurry to get home now, with her burden of news. It seemed to her as if she had been away a long while, so much had happened in the meantime.

At the parsonage gate, Pauline found Patience waiting for her. "You have taken your time, Paul Shaw!" the child said, climbing in beside her sister.

"Fanny's time, you mean!"

"It hasn't come yet!" Patience said protestingly. "I went for the mail myself this afternoon, so I know!"

"Oh, well, perhaps it will to-morrow," Pauline answered, with so little of real concern in her voice, that Patience wondered. "Suppose you take Fanny on to the barn. Mother's home, isn't she?"

Patience glanced at her sharply. "You've got something—particular—to tell mother! O Paul, please wait 'til I come. Is it about—"

"You're getting to look more like an interrogation point every day, Impatience!" Pauline told her, getting down from the gig.

Patience sniffed. "If nobody ever asked questions, nobody'd ever know anything!" she declared.

"Is mother home?" Pauline asked again.

"Who's asking things now!" Patience drew the reins up tightly and bouncing up and down on the carriage seat, called sharply—"Hi yi! Hi yi!"

It was the one method that never failed to rouse Fanny's indignation, producing, for the moment, the desired effect; still, as Pauline said, it was hardly a proceeding that Hilary or she could adopt, or, least of all, their father.

As she trotted briskly off to the barn now, the very tilt of Fanny's ears expressed injured dignity. Dignity was Fanny's strong point; that, and the ability to cover less ground in an afternoon than any other horse in Winton. The small human being at the other end of those taut reins might have known she would have needed no urging barnwards.

"Maybe you don't like it," Patience observed, "but that makes no difference—'s long's it's for your good. You're a very unchristiany horse, Fanny Shaw. And I'll 'hi yi' you every time I get a chance; so now go on."

However Patience was indoors in time to hear all but the very beginning of Pauline's story of her afternoon's experience. "I told you," she broke in, "that I saw a nice girl at church last Sunday—in Mrs. Dobson's pew; and Mrs. Dobson kept looking at her out of the corner of her eyes all the time, 'stead of paying attention to what father was saying; and Miranda says, ten to one, Sally Dobson comes out in—"

"That will do, Patience," her mother said,

"if you are going to interrupt in this fashion, you must run away."

Patience subsided reluctantly, her blue eyes most expressive.

"Isn't it nice for Hilary, mother? Now she'll be contented to stay a week or two, don't you think?" Pauline said.

"I hope so, dear. Yes, it is very nice."

"She was looking better already, mother; brighter, you know."

"Mummy, is asking a perfectly necessary question 'interrupting'?"

"Perhaps not, dear, if there is only one," smiled Mrs. Shaw.

"Mayn't I, please, go with Paul and Hilary when they go to call on that girl?"

"On whom, Patience?"

Patience wriggled impatiently; grown people were certainly very trying at times. "On Paul's and Hilary's new friend, mummy."

"Not the first time, Patience; possibly later—"

Patience shrugged. "By and by," she observed, addressing the room at large, "when Paul and Hilary are married, *I'll* be *Miss*

Shaw! And then—" the thought appeared to give her considerable comfort.

"And maybe, Towser," she confided later, as the two sat together on the side porch, "maybe—some day—you and I'll go to call on them on our own account. I'm not sure it isn't your duty to call on those dogs—you lived here first, and I can't see why it isn't mine—to call on that girl. Father says, we should always hasten to welcome the stranger; and they sound dreadfully interesting."

Towser blinked a sleepy acquiescence. In spite of his years, he still followed blindly where Patience led, though the consequences were frequently disastrous.

It was the next afternoon that Pauline, reading in the garden, heard an eager little voice calling excitedly, "Paul, where are you! It's come! It's come! I brought it up from the office myself!"

Pauline sprang up. "Here I am, Patience! Hurry!"

"Well, I like that!" Patience said, coming across the lawn. "Hurry! Haven't I run every inch of the way home!" She waved the letter above her head—" 'Miss Pauline A. Shaw!' It's type-written! O Paul, aren't you going to read it out here!"

For Pauline, catching the letter from her, had run into the house, crying—"Mother! O Mother Shaw!"

CHAPTER III
UNCLE PAUL'S ANSWER

CHAPTER III

"Mother! O mother, where are you!" Pauline cried, and on Mrs. Shaw's answering from her own room, she ran on up-stairs. "O Mother Shaw! It's come at last!" she announced breathlessly.

"So I thought—when I heard Patience calling just now. Pauline, dear, try not to be too disappointed if—"

"You open it, mother—please! Now it's really come, I'm—afraid to." Pauline held out her letter.

"No, dear, it is addressed to you," Mrs. Shaw answered quietly.

And Pauline, a good deal sobered by the gravity with which her mother had received the news, sat down on the wide window seat, near her mother's chair, tearing open the envelope. As she spread out the heavy businesslike sheet of paper within, a small folded enclosure fell from it into her lap.

"Oh, mother!" Pauline caught up the narrow blue slip. She had never received a check from anyone before. "Mother! listen!" and she read aloud, " 'Pay to the order of Miss Pauline A. Shaw, the sum of twenty-five dollars.' "

Twenty-five dollars! One ought to be able to do a good deal with twenty-five dollars!

"Goodness me!" Patience exclaimed. She had followed her sister up-stairs, after a discreet interval, curling herself up unobtrusively in a big chair just inside the doorway. "Can you do what you like with it, Paul?"

But Pauline was bending over the letter, a bright spot of color on each cheek. Presently, she handed it to her mother. "I wish—I'd never written to him! Read it, mother!"

And Mrs. Shaw read, as follows—

NEW YORK CITY, May 31, 19—.
Miss Pauline A. Shaw,
   Winton, Vt.

MY DEAR NIECE: Yours of May 16th to hand. I am sorry to learn that your sister

Hilary appears to be in such poor health at present. Such being the case, however, it would seem to me that home was the best place for her. I do not at all approve of this modern fashion of running about the country, on any and every pretext. Also, if I remember correctly, your father has frequently described Winton to me as a place of great natural charms, and peculiarly adapted to those suffering from so-called nervous disorders.

Altogether, I do not feel inclined to comply with your request to make it possible for your sister to leave home, in search of change and recreation. Instead, beginning with this letter, I will forward you each month during the summer, the sum of twenty-five dollars, to be used in procuring for your sisters and yourself—I understand, there is a third child—such simple and healthful diversions as your parents may approve, the only conditions I make, being, that at no time shall any of your pleasure trips take you further than ten miles from home, and that you keep me informed, from time to time, how this plan of mine is succeeding.

Trusting this may prove satisfactory,
Very respectfully,
PAUL A. SHAW.

"What do you think, mother?" Pauline asked, as Mrs. Shaw finished reading. "Isn't it a very—queer sort of letter?"

"It is an extremely characteristic one, dear."

"I think," Patience could contain herself no longer, "that you are the inconsideratest persons! You know I'm perfectly wild to know what's in that letter!"

"Run away now, Patience," her mother said. "You shall hear about it later," and when Patience had obeyed—not very willingly, Mrs. Shaw turned again to Pauline. "We must show this to your father, before making any plans in regard to it, dear."

"He's coming now. You show it to him, please, mother."

When her mother had gone down-stairs, Pauline still sat there in the window seat, looking soberly out across the lawn to the village street, with its double rows of tall, old trees. So her flag had served little purpose after all! That change for Hilary was still as uncertain, as much a vague part of the future, as it had ever been.

It seemed to the girl, at the moment, as if

'she fairly hated Winton. As though Hilary and she did not already know every stick and stone in it, had not long ago exhausted all its possibilities!

New people might think it "quaint" and "pretty" but they had not lived here all their lives. And, besides, she had expressly told Uncle Paul that the doctor had said that Hilary needed a change.

She was still brooding over the downfall of her hopes, when her mother called to her from the garden. Pauline went down, feeling that it mattered very little what her father's decision had been—it could make so little difference to them, either way.

Mrs. Shaw was on the bench under the old elm, that stood midway between parsonage and church. She had been rereading Uncle Paul's letter, and to Pauline's wonder, there was something like a smile of amusement in her eyes.

"Well, mother?" the girl asked.

"Well, dear, your father and I have talked the matter over, and we have decided to allow you to accept your uncle's offer."

"But that—hateful condition! How is Hilary to get a chance—here in Winton?"

"Who was it that I heard saying, only this morning, Pauline, that even if Uncle Paul didn't agree, she really believed we might manage to have a very pleasant summer here at home?"

"I know—but still, now that we know definitely—"

"We can go to work definitely to do even better."

"But how, mother!"

"That is what we must think over. Suppose you put your wits to work right now. I must go down to Jane's for a few moments. After all, Pauline, those promised twenty-fives can be used very pleasantly—even in Winton."

"But it will still be Winton."

"Winton may develop some unexplored corners, some new outlooks."

Pauline looked rather doubtful; then, catching sight of a small dejected-looking little figure in the swing, under the big cherry-tree at the foot of the lawn, she asked, "I suppose I may tell Patience now, mother? She really has been very good all this time of waiting."

"She certainly has.   Only, not too many details, Pauline.   Patience is of such a confiding
disposition."

"Patience," Pauline called, "suppose we go
see if there aren't some strawberries ripe?"

Patience ran off for a basket.   Strawberries!   As if she didn't know they were only
a pretext.   Grown people were assuredly
very queer—but sometimes, it was necessary
to humor their little whims and ways.

"I don't believe they are ripe yet," she said,
skipping along beside her sister.   "O Paul,
is it—nice?"

"Mother thinks so!"

"Don't you?"

"Maybe I will—after a while.   Hilary isn't
to go away."

"Is that what you wrote and asked Uncle
Paul?   And didn't you ask for us all to go?"

"Certainly not—we're not sick," said Pauline, laughing.

"Miranda says what Hilary needs is a good
herb tonic!"

"Miranda doesn't know everything."

"What is Uncle Paul going to do then?"

"Send some money every month—to have good times with at home."

"One of those blue paper things?"

"I suppose so," Pauline laughed.

"And *you* don't call that *nice!* Well of all the ungratefullest girls! Is it for us *all* to have good times with? Or just Hilary?"

"All of us. Of course, Hilary must come first."

Patience fairly jumped up and down with excitement. "When will they begin, and what will they be like? O Paul, just think of the good times we've had *without* any money 't all! Aren't we the luckiest girls!"

They had reached the strawberry-bed and Patience dropped down in the grass beside it, her hands clasped around her knees. "Good times in Winton will be a lot better than good times anywhere else. Winton's such a nice sociable place."

Pauline settled herself on the top rail of the fence bordering the garden at the back. Patience's enthusiasm was infectious. "What sort of good times do you mean?" she asked.

"Picnics!"

"We have such a lot of picnics—year after year!"

"A nice picnic is always sort of new. Miranda does put up such beautiful lunches. O Paul, couldn't we afford chocolate layer cake *every* time, now?"

"You goosey!" Pauline laughed again heartily.

"And maybe there'll be an excursion somewhere's, and by'n'by there'll be the town fair. Paul, there's a ripe berry! And another and—"

"See here, hold on, Impatience!" Pauline protested, as the berries disappeared, one after another, down Patience's small throat. "Perhaps, if you stop eating them all, we can get enough for mother's and father's supper."

"Maybe they went and hurried to get ripe for to-night, so we could celebrate," Patience suggested. "Paul, mayn't I go with you next time you go over to The Maples?"

"We'll see what mother says."

"I hate 'we'll see's'!" Patience declared, reaching so far over after a particularly tempting berry, that she lost her balance, and fell face down among them.

"Oh, dear!" she sighed, as her sister came to her assistance, "something always seems to happen clean-apron afternoon! Paul, wouldn't it be a 'good time,' if Miranda would agree not to scold 'bout perfectly unavoidable accidents once this whole summer?"

"Who's to do the deciding as to the un-avoidableness?" Pauline asked. "Come on, Patience, we've got about all the ripe ones, and it must be time for you to lay the supper-table."

"Not laying supper-tables would be another good time," Patience answered. "We did get enough, didn't we? I'll hull them."

"I wonder," Pauline said, more as if speaking to herself, "whether maybe mother wouldn't think it good to have Jane in now and then—for extra work? Not supper-tables, young lady."

"Jane would love it. She likes to work with Miranda—she says Miranda's such a nice lady. Do you think she is, Paul?"

"I'm thinking about other things just now."

"I don't—There's mother. Goodness, Miranda's got the cloth on!" And away sped the child.

To Patience's astonishment, nothing was said at supper, either of Uncle Paul's letter, or the wonderful things it was to lead to. Mr. Shaw kept his wife engaged with parish subjects and Pauline appeared lost in thoughts of her own. Patience fidgeted as openly as she dared. Of all queer grown-ups—and it looked as though most grown-ups were more or less queer—father was certainly the queerest. Of course, he knew about the letter; and how could he go on talking about stupid, uninteresting matters—like the Ladies' Aid and the new hymn books?

Even the first strawberries of the season passed unnoticed, as far as he was concerned, though Mrs. Shaw gave Patience a little smiling nod, in recognition of them.

"Mother," Pauline exclaimed, the moment her father had gone back to his study, "I've been thinking—Suppose we get Hilary to pretend—that coming home is coming to a *new* place? That she is coming to visit us? We'll think up all the interesting things to do, that we can, and the pretty places to show her."

"That would be a good plan, Pauline."

"And if she's company, she'll have to have the spare room," Patience added.

"Jolly for you, Patience!" Pauline said. "Only, mother, Hilary doesn't like the spare room; she says it's the dreariest room in the house."

"If she's company, she'll have to pretend to like it, it wouldn't be good manners not to," Patience observed. The prospect opening out ahead of them seemed full of delightful possibilities. "I hope Miranda catches on to the game, and gives us pound-cake and hot biscuits for supper ever so often, and doesn't call me to do things, when I'm busy entertaining 'the company.'"

"Mother," Pauline broke in— "do keep quiet, Impatience—couldn't we do the spare room over—there's that twenty-five dollars? We've planned it so often."

"We might make some alterations, dear— at least."

"We'll take stock the first thing to-morrow

morning. I suppose we can't really start in before Monday."

"Hardly, seeing that it is Friday night."

They were still talking this new idea over, though Patience had been sent to bed, when Mr. Shaw came in from a visit to a sick parishioner. "We've got the most beautiful scheme on hand, father," Pauline told him, wheeling forward his favorite chair. She hoped he would sit down and talk things over with them, instead of going on to the study; it wouldn't be half as nice, if he stayed outside of everything.

"New schemes appear to be rampant these days," Mr. Shaw said, but he settled himself comfortably in the big chair, quite as though he meant to stay with them. "What is this particular one?"

He listened, while Pauline explained, really listened, instead of merely seeming to. "It does appear an excellent idea," he said; "but why should it be Hilary only, who is to try to see Winton with new eyes this summer? Suppose we were all to do so?"

Pauline clapped her hands softly. "Then

you'll help us? And we'll all pretend. May-be Uncle Paul's thought isn't such a bad one, after all."

"Paul always believed in developing the op-portunities nearest hand," Mr. Shaw an-swered. He stroked the head Towser laid against his knee. "Your mother and I will be the gainers—if we keep all our girls at home, and still achieve the desired end."

Pauline glanced up quickly. How could she have thought him unheeding—indifferent?

"Somehow, I think it will work out all right," she said. "Anyhow, we're going to try it, aren't we, Mother Shaw? Patience thinks it the best idea ever, there'll be no urging needed there."

Pauline went up to bed that night feel-ing strangely happy. For one thing the un-certainty was over, and if they set to work to make this summer full of interest, to break up the monotony and routine that Hilary found so irksome, the result must be satisfactory. And lastly, there was the comforting convic-tion, that whatever displeasure her father had felt at first, at her taking the law into her own hands in such unforeseen fashion, had disappeared now; and he was not going to stay "outside of things," that was sure.

The next morning, as soon as breakfast was over, Pauline ran up-stairs to the spare room. She threw open the shutters of the four windows, letting in the fresh morning air. The side windows faced west, and looked out across the pleasant tree-shaded yard to the church; those at the front faced south, overlooking the broad village street.

In the bright sunlight, the big square room stood forth in all its prim orderliness. "It is ugly," Pauline decided, shaking her head disapprovingly, but it had possibilities. No room, with four such generous windows and —for the fire-board must come out—such a wide deep fireplace, could be without them.

She turned, as her mother came in, duly attended by Patience. "It is hideous, isn't it, mother? The paper, I mean—and the carpet isn't much better. It did very well, I suppose, for the visiting ministers—probably they're too busy thinking over their sermons to notice —but for Hilary—"

Mrs. Shaw smiled. "Perhaps you are right, dear. As to the unattractiveness of the paper—"

"We must repaper—that's sure; plain green, with a little touch of color in the border, and, oh, Mother Shaw, wouldn't a green and white matting be lovely?"

"And expensive, Pauline."

"It wouldn't take all the twenty-five, I'm sure. Miranda'll do the papering, I know. She did the study last year. Mother, couldn't we have Jane in for the washing and ironing this week, and let Miranda get right at this room? I'll help with the ironing, too."

"I suppose so, dear. Miranda is rather fussy about letting other people do her regular work, you know."

"I'll ask her."

"And remember, Pauline, each day is going to bring new demands—don't put all your eggs into one basket."

"I won't. We needn't spend anything on this room except for the paper and matting."

Half an hour later, Pauline was on her way down to the village store for samples of paper. She had already settled the matter with Miranda, over the wiping of the breakfast dishes.

Miranda had lived with the Shaws ever since Pauline was a baby, and was a very important member of the family, both in her own and their opinion. She was tall and gaunt, and somewhat severe looking; however, in her case, looks were deceptive. It would never have occurred to Miranda that the Shaws' interests were not her interests—she considered herself an important factor in the upbringing of the three young people. If she had a favorite, it was probably Hilary.

"Hmn," she said, when Pauline broached the subject of the spare room, "what put that notion in your head, I'd like to know! That paper ain't got a tear in it!"

So Pauline went further, telling her something of Uncle Paul's letter and how they hoped to carry his suggestion out.

Miranda stood still, her hands in the dish water—"That's your pa's own brother, ain't it?"

Pauline nodded. "And Miranda—"

"I reckon he ain't much like the minister. Well, me an' Sarah Jane ain't the least bit alike—if we are sisters. I guess I can manage 'bout the papering. But it does go 'gainst me, having that sexton woman in. Still, I reckon you can't be content, 'till we get started. Looking for the old gentleman up, later, be you?"

"For whom?" Pauline asked.

"Your pa's brother. The minister's getting on, and the other one's considerable older, I understand."

"I don't think he will be up," Pauline answered; she hadn't thought of that before. Suppose he should come! She wondered what he would be like.

Half way down the street, Pauline was overtaken by her younger sister. "Are you going to get the new things now, Paul?" she asked eagerly.

"Of course not, just get some samples."

"There's always such a lot of getting ready first," Patience sighed. "Paul, mother says I may go with you to-morrow afternoon."

"All right," Pauline agreed. "Only, you've

got to promise not to 'hi yi' at Fanny all the way."

"I won't—all the way."

"And—Impatience?"

"Yes?"

"You needn't say what we want the new paper for, or anything about what we are planning to do—in the store I mean."

"Mr. Ward would be mighty interested."

"I dare say."

"Miranda says you're beginning to put on considerable airs, since you've been turning your hair up, Paul Shaw. When I put my hair up, I'm going on being just as nice and friendly with folks, as before, you'll see."

Pauline laughed, which was not at all to Patience's liking. "All the same, mind what I say," she warned.

"Can I help choose?" Patience asked, as they reached the store.

"If you like." Pauline went through to the little annex devoted to wall papers and carpetings. It was rather musty and dull in there, Patience thought; she would have liked to make a slow round of the whole store, ex-

changing greetings and various confidences
with the other occupants. The store was a
busy place on Saturday morning, and Patience knew every man, woman and child in
Winton.

They had got their samples and Pauline was
lingering before a new line of summer dress-
goods just received, when the young fellow in
charge of the post-office and telegraph station
called to her: "I say, Miss Shaw, here's a message just come for you."

"For me—" Pauline took it wonderingly.
Her hands were trembling, she had never received a telegram before—Was Hilary? Then
she laughed at herself. To have sent a message, Mr. Boyd would have first been obliged
to come in to Winton.

Out on the sidewalk, she tore open the envelope, not heeding Patience's curious demands. It was from her uncle, and read—

"Have some one meet the afternoon train
Saturday, am sending you an aid towards your
summer's outings."

"Oh," Pauline said, "do hurry, Patience. I
want to get home as fast as I can."

CHAPTER IV

BEGINNINGS

CHAPTER IV

BEGINNINGS

SUNDAY afternoon, Pauline and Patience drove over to The Maples to see Hilary. They stopped, as they went by, at the post-office for Pauline to mail a letter to her uncle, which was something in the nature of a very enthusiastic postscript to the one she had written him Friday night, acknowledging and thanking him for his cheque, and telling him of the plans already under discussion.

"And now," Patience said, as they turned out of the wide main street, "we're really off. I reckon Hilary'll be looking for us, don't you?"

"I presume she will," Pauline answered.

"Maybe she'll want to come back with us."

"Oh, I don't believe so. She knows mother wants her to stay the week out. Listen, Patty—"

Patience sat up and took notice. When people Pattied her, it generally meant they had a favor to ask, or something of the sort.

"Remember, you're to be very careful not to let Hilary suspect—anything."

"About the room and—?"

"I mean—everything."

"Won't she like it—all, when she does know?"

"Well, rather!"

Patience wriggled excitedly. "It's like having a fairy godmother, isn't it? And three wishes? If you'd had three wishes, Paul, wouldn't you've chosen—"

"You'd better begin quieting down, Patience, or Hilary can't help suspecting something."

Patience drew a long breath. "If she knew —she wouldn't stay a single day longer, would she?"

"That's one reason why she mustn't know."

"When will you tell her; or is mother going to?"

"I don't know yet. See here, Patience, you may drive—if you won't hi yi."

"Please, Paul, let me, when we get to the avenue. It's stupid coming to a place, like Fanny'd gone to sleep."

"Not before—and only once then," Pauline stipulated, and Patience possessed her soul in at least a faint semblance of patience until they turned into the avenue of maples. Then she suddenly tightened her hold on the reins, bounced excitedly up and down, crying sharply—"Hi yi!"

Fanny instantly pricked up her ears, and, what was more to the purpose, actually started into what might almost have been called a trot. "There! you see!" Patience said proudly, as they turned into the yard.

Hilary came down the porch steps. "I heard Impatience urging her Rosinante on," she laughed. "Why didn't you let her drive all the way, Paul? I've been watching for you since dinner."

"We've been pretty nearly since dinner getting here, it seems to me," Patience declared. "We had to wait for Paul to write a letter first to—"

"Are you alone?" Pauline broke in hurriedly, asking the first question that came into her mind.

Hilary smiled ruefully. "Not exactly. Mr. Boyd's asleep in the sitting-room, and Mrs. Boyd's taking a nap up-stairs in her own room."

"You poor child!" Pauline said. "Jump out, Patience!"

"*Have* you brought me something to read? I've finished both the books I brought with me, and gone through a lot of magazines— queer old things, that Mrs. Boyd took years and years ago."

"Then you've done very wrong," Pauline told her severely, leading Fanny over to a shady spot at one side of the yard and tying her to the fence—a quite unnecessary act, as nothing would have induced Fanny to take her departure unsolicited.

"Guess!" Pauline came back, carrying a small paper-covered parcel. "Father sent it to you. He was over at Vergennes yesterday."

"Oh!" Hilary cried, taking it eagerly and sitting down on the steps. "It's a book, of

course." Even more than her sisters, she had
inherited her father's love of books, and a new
book was an event at the parsonage. "Oh,"
she cried again, taking off the paper and dis-
closing the pretty tartan cover within, "O
Paul! It's 'Penelope's Progress.' Don't you
remember those bits we read in those odd
magazines Josie lent us? And how we
wanted to read it all?"

Pauline nodded. "I reckon mother told father about it; I saw her following him out to
the gig yesterday morning."

They went around to the little porch leading
from Hilary's room, always a pleasant spot in
the afternoons.

"Why," Patience exclaimed, "it's like an
out-door parlor, isn't it?"

There was a big braided mat on the floor
of the porch, its colors rather faded by time
and use, but looking none the worse for that,
a couple of rockers, a low stool, and a small
table, covered with a bit of bright cretonne.
On it stood a blue and white pitcher filled with
field flowers, beside it lay one or two magazines. Just outside, extending from one of the

porch posts to the limb of an old cherry tree, hung Hilary's hammock, gay with cushions.

"Shirley did it yesterday afternoon," Hilary explained. "She was over here a good while. Mrs. Boyd let us have the things and the chintz for the cushions, Shirley made them, and we filled them with hay."

Pauline, sitting on the edge of the low porch, looked about her with appreciative eyes. "How pleasant and cozy it is, and after all, it only took a little time and trouble."

Hilary laid her new book on the table. "How soon do you suppose we can go over to the manor, Paul? I imagine the Dayres have fixed it up mighty pretty. Mr. Dayre was over here, last night. He and Shirley are ever so—chummy. He's Shirley Putnam Dayre, and she's Shirley Putnam Dayre, Junior. So he calls her 'Junior' and she calls him 'Senior.' They're just like brother and sister. He's an artist, they've been everywhere together. And, Paul, they think Winton is delightful. Mr. Dayre says the village street, with its great overhanging trees, and old-fashioned houses, is a picture in itself, particularly up at our

end, with the church, all ivy-covered. He
means to paint the church sometime this summer."

"It would make a pretty picture," Pauline
said thoughtfully. "Hilary, I wonder—"

"So do I," Hilary said. "Still, after all,
one would like to see different places—"

"And love only one," Pauline added; she
turned to her sister. "You are better, aren't
you—already?"

"I surely am. Shirley's promised to take
me out on the lake soon. She's going to be
friends with us, Paul—really friends. She
says we must call her 'Shirley,' that she doesn't
like 'Miss Dayre,' she hears it so seldom."

"I think it's nice—being called 'Miss,' " Patience remarked, from where she had curled
herself up in the hammock. "I suppose she
doesn't want it, because she can have it—I'd
love to be called 'Miss Shaw.' "

"Hilary," Pauline said, "would you mind
very much, if you couldn't go away this summer?"

"It wouldn't do much good if I did, would
it?"

"The not minding would—to mother and the rest of us—"

"And if you knew what—" Patience began excitedly.

"Don't you want to go find Captain, Impatience?" Pauline asked hastily, and Patience, feeling that she had made a false move, went with most unusual meekness.

"Know what?" Hilary asked.

"I—shouldn't wonder, if the child had some sort of scheme on hand," Pauline said, she hoped she wasn't—prevaricating; after all, Patience probably did have some scheme in her head—she usually had.

"I haven't thought much about going away the last day or so," Hilary said. "I suppose it's the feeling better, and, then, the getting to know Shirley."

"I'm glad of that." Pauline sat silent for some moments; she was watching a fat bumble bee buzzing in and out among the flowers in the garden. It was always still, over here at the farm, but to-day, it seemed a different sort of stillness, as if bees and birds and flowers knew that it was Sunday afternoon.

"Paul," Hilary asked suddenly, "what are you smiling to yourself about?"

"Was I smiling? I didn't know it. I guess because it is so nice and peaceful here and because—Hilary, let's start a club—the 'S. W. F. Club.'"

"The what?"

"The 'S. W. F. Club.' No, I shan't tell you what the letters stand for! You've got to think it out for yourself."

"A real club, Paul?"

"Indeed, yes."

"Who's to belong?"

"Oh, lots of folks. Josie and Tom, and you and I—and I think, maybe, mother and father."

"Father! To belong to a club!"

"It was he who put the idea into my head."

Hilary came to sit beside her sister on the step. "Paul, I've a feeling that there is something—up! And it isn't the barometer!"

"Where did you get it?"

"From you."

Pauline sprang up. "Feelings are very unreliable things to go by, but I've one just now

—that if we don't hunt Impatience up pretty
quick—there will be something doing."

They found Patience sitting on the barn
floor, utterly regardless of her white frock.   A
whole family of kittens were about her.

"Aren't they dears!" Patience demanded.

"Mrs. Boyd says I may have my choice, to
take home with me," Hilary said.   The parsonage cat had died the fall before, and had
had no successor as yet.

Patience held up a small coal-black one.
"Choose this, Hilary!   Miranda says a black
cat brings luck, though it don't look like we
needed any black cats to bring—"

"I like the black and white one," Pauline
interposed, just touching Patience with the
tip of her shoe.

"Maybe Mrs. Boyd would give us each one,
that would leave one for her," Patience suggested cheerfully.

"I imagine mother would have something
to say to that," Pauline told her.   "Was Josie
over yesterday, Hilary?"

Hilary nodded.   "In the morning."

As they were going back to the house, they

met Mr. Boyd, on his way to pay his regular weekly visit to the far pasture.

"Going to salt the colts?" Patience asked. "Please, mayn't I come?"

"There won't be time, Patience," Pauline said.

"Not time!" Mr. Boyd objected, "I'll be back to supper, and you girls are going to stay to supper." He carried Patience off with him, declaring that he wasn't sure he should let her go home at all, he meant to keep her altogether some day, and why not to-night?

"Oh, I couldn't stay to-night," the child assured him earnestly. "Of course, I couldn't ever stay for always, but by'n'by, when—there isn't so much going on at home—there's such a lot of things keep happening at home now, only don't tell Hilary, please—maybe, I could come make you a truly visit."

Indoors, Pauline and Hilary found Mrs. Boyd down-stairs again from her nap. "You ain't come after Hilary?" she questioned anxiously.

"Only to see her," Pauline answered, and while she helped Mrs. Boyd get supper, she confided to her the story of Uncle Paul's letter and the plans already under way.

Mrs. Boyd was much interested. "Bless me, it'll do her a heap of good, you'll see, my dear. I'm not sure, I don't agree with your uncle, when all's said and done, home's the best place for young folks."

Just before Pauline and Patience went home that evening, Mrs. Boyd beckoned Pauline mysteriously into the best parlor. "I always meant her to have them some day—she being my god-child—and maybe they'll do her as much good now, as any time, she'll want to fix up a bit now and then, most likely. Shirley had on a string of them last night, but not to compare with these." Mrs. Boyd was kneeling before a trunk in the parlor closet, and presently she put a little square shell box into Pauline's hands. "Box and all, just like they came to me—you know, they were my grandmother's—but Hilary's a real careful sort of girl."

"But, Mrs. Boyd—I'm not sure that mother would—" Pauline knew quite well what was in the box.

"That's all right! You just slip them in Hilary's top drawer, where she'll come across them without expecting it. Deary me, I never wear them, and as I say, I've always meant to give them to her some day."

"She'll be perfectly delighted—and they'll look so pretty. Hilary's got a mighty pretty neck, I think." Pauline went out to the gig, the little box hidden carefully in her blouse, feeling that Patience was right and that these were very fairy-story sort of days.

"You'll be over again soon, won't you?" Hilary urged.

"We're going to be tre-men-dous-ly busy," Patience began, but her sister cut her short.

"As soon as I can, Hilary. Mind you go on getting better."

By Monday noon, the spare room had lost its look of prim order. In the afternoon, Pauline and her mother went down to the store to buy the matting. There was not much choice to be had, and the only green and white there was, was considerably beyond the limit they had allowed themselves.

"Never mind," Pauline said cheerfully, "plain white will look ever so cool and pretty —perhaps, the green would fade. I'm going to believe so."

Over a low wicker sewing-chair, she did linger longingly; it would look so nice beside one of the west windows. She meant to place a low table for books and work between those side windows. In the end, prudence won the day, and surely, the new paper and matting were enough to be grateful for in themselves.

By the next afternoon the paper was on and the matting down. Pauline was up garret rummaging, when she heard someone calling her from the foot of the stairs. "I'm here, Josie," she called back, and her friend came running up.

"What *are* you doing?" she asked.

Pauline held up an armful of old-fashioned chintz.

"Oh, how pretty!" Josie exclaimed. "It makes one think of high-waisted dresses, and minuets and things like that."

Pauline laughed. "They were my great-grandmother's bed curtains."

"Goodness! What are you going to do with them?"

"I'm not sure mother will let me do anything. I came across them just now in looking for some green silk she said I might have to cover Hilary's pin-cushion with."

"For the new room? Patience has been doing the honors of the new paper and matting —it's going to be lovely, I think."

Pauline scrambled to her feet, shaking out the chintz: "If only mother would—it's pink and green—let's go ask her."

"What do you want to do with it, Pauline?" Mrs. Shaw asked.

"I haven't thought that far—use it for draperies of some kind, I suppose," the girl answered.

They were standing in the middle of the big, empty room. Suddenly, Josie gave a quick exclamation, pointing to the bare corner between the front and side windows. "Wouldn't a cozy corner be delightful—with cover and cushions of the chintz?"

"May we, mother?" Pauline begged in a coaxing tone.

"I suppose so, dear—only where is the bench part to come from?"

"Tom'll make the frame for it, I'll go get him this minute," Josie answered.

"And you might use that single mattress from up garret," Mrs. Shaw suggested.

Pauline ran up to inspect it. and to see what other treasures might be forthcoming. The garret was a big, shadowy place, extending over the whole house, and was lumber room, play place and general refuge, all in one.

Presently, from under the eaves, she drew forward a little old-fashioned sewing-chair, discarded on the giving out of its cane seat. "But I could tack a piece of burlap on and cover it with a cushion," Pauline decided, and bore it down in triumph to the new room, where Tom Brice was already making his measurements for the cozy corner.

Josie was on the floor, measuring for the cover. "Isn't it fun, Paul? Tom says it won't take long to do his part."

Tom straightened himself, slipping his rule into his pocket. "I don't see what you want it for, though," he said.

"'Yours not to reason why—'" Pauline told him. "We see, and so will Hilary. Don't you and Josie want to join the new club—the 'S. W. F. Club'?"

"Society of Willing Females, I suppose?" Tom remarked.

"It sounds like some sort of sewing circle," Josie said.

Pauline sat down in one of the wide window places. "I'm not sure it might not take in both. It is—'The Seeing Winton First Club.'"

Josie looked as though she didn't quite understand, but Tom whistled softly. "What else have you been doing for the past fifteen years, if you please, ma'am?" he asked quizzically.

Pauline laughed. "One ought to know a place rather thoroughly in fifteen years, I suppose; but—I'm hoping we can make it seem at least a little bit new and different this summer—for Hilary. You see, we shan't be able to send her away, and so, I thought, perhaps, if we tried looking at Winton—with new eyes—"

"I see," Josie cried. "I think it's a splen-diferous idea!"

"And, I thought, if we formed a sort of club among ourselves and worked together—"

"Listen," Josie interrupted again, "we'll make it a condition of membership, that each one must, in turn, think up something pleasant to do."

"Is the membership to be limited?" Tom asked.

Pauline smiled. "It will be so—necessarily —won't it?" For Winton was not rich in young people.

"There will be enough of us," Josie declared hopefully.

"Like the model dinner party?" her brother asked. "Not less than the Graces, nor more than the Muses."

And so the new club was formed then and there. There were to be no regular and formal meetings, no dues, nor fines, and each member was to consider himself, or herself, an active member of the programme committee.

Tom, as the oldest member of their immediate circle of friends, was chosen president before that first meeting adjourned; no other officers were considered necessary at the time. And being president, to him was promptly delegated the honor—despite his vigorous protests—of arranging for their first outing and notifying the other members—yet to be.

"But," he expostulated, "what's a fellow to think up—in a hole like this?"

"Winton isn't a hole!" his sister protested. It was one of the chief occupations of Josie's life at present, to contradict all such heretical utterances on Tom's part. He was to go away that fall to commence his studies for the medical profession, for it was Dr. Brice's great desire that, later, his son should assist him in his practice. But, so far, Tom though wanting to follow his father's profession, was firm in his determination, not to follow it in Winton.

"And remember," Pauline said, as the three went down-stairs together, "that it's the first step that counts—and to think up something very delightful, Tom."

"It mustn't be a picnic, I suppose? Hilary won't be up to picnics yet awhile."

"N-no, and we want to begin soon. She'll be back Friday, I think," Pauline answered.

By Wednesday night the spare room was ready for the expected guest. "It's as if someone had waved a fairy wand over it, isn't it?" Patience said delightedly. "Hilary'll be so surprised."

"I think she will and—pleased." Pauline gave one of the cushions in the cozy corner a straightening touch, and drew the window shades—Miranda had taken them down and turned them—a little lower.

"It's a regular company room, isn't it?" Patience said joyously.

The minister drove over to The Maples himself on Friday afternoon to bring Hilary home.

"Remember," Patience pointed a warning forefinger at him, just as he was starting, "not a single solitary hint!"

"Not a single solitary one," he promised.

As he turned out of the gate, Patience drew a long breath. "Well, he's off at last! But, oh, dear, however can we wait 'til he gets back?"

CHAPTER V
BEDELIA

CHAPTER V

BEDELIA

IT was five o'clock that afternoon when Patience, perched, a little white-clad sentry, on the gate-post, announced joyously—"They're coming! They're coming!"

Patience was as excited as if the expected "guest" were one in fact, as well as name. It was fun to be playing a game of make-believe, in which the elders took part.

As the gig drew up before the steps, Hilary looked eagerly out. "Will you tell me," she demanded, "why father insisted on coming 'round the lower road, by the depot—he didn't stop, and he didn't get any parcel? And when I asked him, he just laughed and looked mysterious."

"He went," Pauline answered, "because we asked him to—company usually comes by train —real out-of-town company, you know."

"Like visiting ministers and returned missionaries," Patience explained.

Hilary looked thoroughly bewildered. "But are you expecting company? You must be," she glanced from one to another, "you're all dressed up."

"We were expecting some, dear," her mother told her, "but she has arrived."

"Don't you see? You're it!" Patience danced excitedly about her sister.

"I'm the company!" Hilary said wonderingly. Then her eyes lighted up. "I understand! How perfectly dear of you all."

Mrs. Shaw patted the hand Hilary slipped into hers. "You have come back a good deal better than you went, my dear. The change has done you good."

"And it didn't turn out a stupid—half-way affair, after all," Hilary declared. "I've had a lovely time. Only, I simply had to come home, I felt somehow—that—that—"

"We were expecting company?" Pauline laughed. "And you wanted to be here?"

"I reckon that was it," Hilary agreed. As she sat there, resting a moment, before going up-stairs, she hardly seemed the same girl who had gone away so reluctantly only eight days before. The change of scene, the out-door life, the new friendship, bringing with it new interests, had worked wonders.

"And now," Pauline suggested, taking up her sister's valise, "perhaps you would like to go up to your room—visitors generally do."

"To rest after your journey, you know," Patience prompted. Patience believed in playing one's part down to the minutest detail.

"Thank you," Hilary answered, with quite the proper note of formality in her voice, "if you don't mind; though I did not find the trip as fatiguing as I had expected."

But from the door, she turned back to give her mother a second and most uncompany-like hug. "It is good to be home, Mother Shaw! And please, you don't want to pack me off again anywhere right away—at least, all by myself?"

"Not right away," her mother answered, kissing her.

"I guess you will think it is good to be

home, when you know—everything," Patience announced, accompanying her sisters up-stairs, but on the outside of the banisters.

"Patty!" Pauline protested laughingly— "Was there ever such a child for letting things out!"

"I haven't!" the child exclaimed, "only now —it can't make any difference."

"There is mystery in the very air!" Hilary insisted. "Oh, what have you all been up to?"

"You're not to go in there!" Patience cried, as Hilary stopped before the door of her own and Pauline's room.

"Of course you're not," Pauline told her. "It strikes me, for company—you're making yourself very much at home! Walking into peoples' rooms." She led the way along the hall to the spare room, throwing the door wide open.

"Oh!" Hilary cried, then stood quite still on the threshold, looking about her with wide, wondering eyes.

The spare room was grim and gray no longer. Hilary felt as if she must be in some strange, delightful dream. The cool green of

the wall paper, with the soft touch of pink in
ceiling and border, the fresh white matting,
the cozy corner opposite—with its delicate old-
fashioned chintz drapery and big cushions, the
new toilet covers—white over green, the fresh
curtains at the windows, the cushioned window seats, the low table and sewing-chair,
even her own narrow white bed, with its new
ruffled spread, all went to make a room as
strange to her, as it was charming and unexpected.

"Oh," she said again, turning to her mother,
who had followed them up-stairs, and stood
waiting just outside the door. "How perfectly lovely it all is—but it isn't for me?"

"Of course it is," Patience said. "Aren't
you company—you aren't just Hilary now,
you're 'Miss Shaw' and you're here on a visit;
and there's company asked to supper to-morrow night, and it's going to be such fun!"

Hilary's color came and went. It was
something deeper and better than fun. She
understood now why they had done this—why
Pauline had said that—about her not going
away; there was a sudden lump in the girl's

throat—she was glad, so glad, she had said that down-stairs—about not wanting to go away.

And when her mother and Patience had gone down-stairs again and Pauline had begun to unpack the valise, as she had unpacked it a week ago at The Maples, Hilary sat in the low chair by one of the west windows, her hands folded in her lap, looking about this new room of hers.

"There," Pauline said presently, "I believe that's all now—you'd better lie down, Hilary —I'm afraid you're tired."

"No, I'm not; at any rate, not very. I'll lie down if you like, only I know I shan't be able to sleep."

Pauline lowered the pillow and threw a light cover over her. "There's something in the top drawer of the dresser," she said, "but you're not to look at it until you've lain down at least half an hour."

"I feel as if I were in an enchanted palace," Hilary said, "with so many delightful surprises being sprung on me all the while." After Pauline had gone, she lay watching the slight swaying of the wild roses in the tall jar on the hearth. The wild roses ran rampant in the little lane leading from the back of the church down past the old cottage where Sextoness Jane lived. Jane had brought these with her that morning, as her contribution to the new room.

To Hilary, as to Patience, it seemed as if a magic wand had been waved, transforming the old dull room into a place for a girl to live and dream in. But for her, the name of the wand was Love.

There must be no more impatient longings, no fretful repinings, she told herself now. She must not be slow to play her part in this new game that had been originated all for her.

The half-hour up, she slipped from the bed and began unbuttoning her blue-print frock. Being company, it stood to reason she must dress for supper. But first, she must find out what was in the upper drawer.

The first glimpse of the little shell box, told her that. There were tears in Hilary's gray eyes, as she stood slipping the gold beads slowly through her fingers. How good everyone was to her; for the first time some under-standing of the bright side even of sickness—and she had not been really sick, only run-down—and, yes, she had been cross and hor-rid, lots of times—came to her.

"I'll go over just as soon as I can and thank her," the girl thought, clasping the beads about her neck, "and I'll keep them always and al-ways."

A little later, she came down-stairs all in white, a spray of the pink and white wild roses in her belt, her soft, fair hair freshly brushed and braided. She had been rather neglectful of her hair lately.

There was no one on the front piazza but her father, and he looked up from his book with a smile of pleasure. "My dear, how well you are looking! It is certainly good to see you at home again, and quite your old self."

Hilary came to sit on the arm of his chair. "It is good to be at home again. I suppose you know all the wonderful surprises I found waiting me?"

"Supper's ready," Patience proclaimed

from the doorway. "Please come, because—" she caught herself up, putting a hand into Hilary's, "I'll show you where to sit, Miss Shaw."

Hilary laughed. "How old are you, my dear?" she asked, in the tone frequently used by visiting ministers.

"I'm a good deal older than I'm treated generally," Patience answered. "Do you like Winton?"

"I am sure I shall like it very much." Hilary slipped into the chair Patience drew forward politely. "The company side of the table—sure enough," she laughed.

"It isn't proper to say things to yourself sort of low down in your voice," Patience reproved her, then at a warning glance from her mother subsided into silence as the minister took his place.

For to-night, at least, Miranda had amply fulfilled Patience's hopes, as to company suppers. And she, too, played her part in the new game, calling Hilary "Miss," and never by any chance intimating that she had seen her before.

"Did you go over to the manor to see Shirley?" Patience asked.

Hilary shook her head. "I promised her Pauline and I would be over soon. We may have Fanny some afternoon, mayn't we, father?"

Patience's blue eyes danced. "They can't have Fanny, can they, father?" she nodded at him knowingly.

Hilary eyed her questioningly. "What *is* the matter, Patience?"

"Nothing is the matter with her," Pauline said hurriedly. "Don't pay any attention to her."

"Only, if you would hurry," Patience implored. "I—I can't wait much longer!"

"Wait!" Hilary asked. "For what?"

Patience pushed back her chair. "For— Well, if you just knew what for, Hilary Shaw, you'd do some pretty tall hustling!"

"Patience!" her father said reprovingly.

"May I be excused, mother?" Patience asked. "I'll wait out on the porch."

And Mrs. Shaw replied most willingly that she might.

"Is there anything more—to see, I mean, not to eat?" Hilary asked. "I don't see how there can be."

"Are you through?" Pauline answered. "Because, if you are, I'll show you."

"It was sent to Paul," Patience called, from the hall door. "But she says, of course, it was meant for us all; and I think, myself, she's right about that."

"Is it—alive?" Hilary asked.

" 'It' was—before supper," Pauline told her. "I certainly hope nothing has happened to—'it' since then."

"A dog?" Hilary suggested.

"Wait and see; by the way, where's that kitten?"

"She's to follow in a few days; she was a bit too young to leave home just yet."

"I've got the sugar!" Patience called.

Hilary stopped short at the foot of the porch steps. Patience's remark, if it had not absolutely let the cat out of the bag, had at least opened the bag. "Paul, it can't be—"

"In the Shaw's dictionary, at present, there doesn't appear to be any such word as can't,"

Pauline declared. "Come on—after all, you know, the only way to find out—is to find out."

Patience had danced on ahead down the path to the barn. She stood waiting for them now in the broad open doorway, her whole small person one animated exclamation point, while Towser, just home from a leisurely round of afternoon visits, came forward to meet Hilary, wagging a dignified welcome.

"If you don't hurry, I'll 'hi yi' you, like I do Fanny!" Patience warned them. She moved to one side, to let Hilary go on into the barn. "Now!" she demanded, "isn't that something more?"

From the stall beside Fanny's, a horse's head reached inquiringly out for the sugar with which already she had come to associate the frequent visits of these new friends. She was a pretty, well-made, little mare, light sorrel, with white markings, and with a slender, intelligent face.

Hilary stood motionless, too surprised to speak.

"Her name's Bedelia," Patience said, doing the honors. "She's very clever, she knows us all already. Fanny hasn't been very polite to her, and she knows it—Bedelia does, I mean —sometimes, when Fanny isn't looking, I've caught Bedelia sort of laughing at her—and I don't blame her one bit. And, oh, Hilary, she *can* go—there's no need to 'hi yi' *her.*"

"But—" Hilary turned to Pauline.

"Uncle Paul sent her," Pauline explained. "She came last Saturday afternoon. One of the men from Uncle Paul's place in the country brought her. She was born and bred at River Lawn—that's Uncle Paul's place—he says."

Hilary stroked the glossy neck gently, if Pauline had said the Sultan of Turkey, instead of Uncle Paul, she could hardly have been more surprised. "Uncle Paul—sent her to you!" she said slowly.

"To *us.*"

"Bless me, that isn't all he sent," Patience exclaimed. It seemed to Patience that they never would get to the end of their story. "You just come look at this, Hilary Shaw!"

she ran on through the opening connecting carriage-house with stable.

"Oh!" Hilary cried, following with Pauline.

Beside the minister's shabby old gig, stood the smartest of smart traps, and hanging on the wall behind it, a pretty russet harness, with silver mountings.

Hilary sat down on an old saw horse; she felt again as though she must be dreaming.

"There isn't another such cute rig in town, Jim says so," Patience said. Jim was the stable boy. "It beats Bell Ward's all to pieces."

"But why—I mean, how did Uncle Paul ever come to send it to us?" Hilary said. Of course one had always known that there was —somewhere—a person named Uncle Paul; but he had appeared about as remote and indefinite a being as—that same Sultan of Turkey, for instance.

"After all, why shouldn't he?" Pauline answered.

"But I don't believe he would've if Paul had not written to him that time," Patience added. "Maybe next time I tell you anything, you'll believe me, Hilary Shaw."

But Hilary was staring at Pauline. "You didn't write to Uncle Paul?"

"I'm afraid I did."

"Was—was that the letter—you remember, that afternoon?"

"I rather think I do remember."

"Paul, how did you ever dare?"

"I was in the mood to dare anything that day."

"And did he answer; but of course he did."

"Yes—he answered. Though not right away."

"Was it a nice letter? Did he mind your having written? Paul, you didn't ask him to send you—these," Hilary waved her hand rather vaguely.

"Hardly—he did that all on his own. It wasn't a bad sort of letter, I'll tell you about it by and by. We can go to the manor in style now, can't we—even if father can't spare Fanny. Bedelia's perfectly gentle, I've driven her a little ways once or twice, to make sure. Father insisted on going with me.

We created quite a sensation down street, I assure you."

"And Mrs. Dane said," Patience cut in, "that in her young days, clergymen didn't go kiting 'bout the country in such high-fangled rigs."

"Never mind what Mrs. Dane said, or didn't say," Pauline told her.

"Miranda says, what Mrs. Dane hasn't got to say on any subject, wouldn't make you tired listening to it."

"Patience, if you don't stop repeating what everyone says, I shall—"

"If you speak to mother—then you'll be repeating," Patience declared. "Maybe, I oughtn't to have said those things before—company."

"I think we'd better go back to the house now," Pauline suggested.

"Sextoness Jane says," Patience remarked, "that she'd have sure admired to have a horse and rig like that, when she was a girl. She says, she doesn't suppose you'll be passing by her house very often."

"And, now, please," Hilary pleaded, when

she had been established in her hammock on the side porch, with her mother in her chair close by, and Pauline sitting on the steps, "I want to hear—everything. I'm what Miranda calls 'fair mazed.' "

So Pauline told nearly everything, blurring some of the details a little and getting to that twenty-five dollars a month, with which they were to do so much, as quickly as possible.

"O Paul, really," Hilary sat up among her cushions—"Why, it'll be—riches, won't it?"

"It seems so."

"But—Oh, I'm afraid you've spent all the first twenty-five on me; and that's not a fair division—is it, Mother Shaw?"

"We used it quite according to Hoyle," Pauline insisted. "We got our fun that way, didn't we, Mother Shaw?"

Their mother smiled. "I know I did."

"All the same, after this, you've simply got to 'drink fair, Betsy,' so remember," Hilary warned them.

"Bedtime, Patience," Mrs. Shaw said, and Patience got slowly out of her big, wicker armchair.

"I did think—seeing there was company,—that probably you'd like me to stay up a little later to-night."

"If the 'company' takes my advice, she'll go, too," her mother answered.

"The 'company' thinks she will." Hilary slipped out of the hammock. "Mother, do you suppose Miranda's gone to bed yet?"

"I'll go see," Patience offered, willing to postpone the inevitable for even those few moments longer.

"What do you want with Miranda?" Pauline asked.

"To do something for me."

"Can't I do it?"

"No—and it must be done to-night. Mother, what are you smiling over?"

"I thought it would be that way, dear."

"Miranda's coming," Patience called. "She'd just taken her back hair down, and she's waiting to twist it up again. She's got awful funny back hair."

"Patience! Patience!" her mother said reprovingly.

"I mean, there's such a little—"

"Go up-stairs and get yourself ready for bed at once."

Miranda was waiting in the spare room. "You ain't took sick, Hilary?"

Hilary shook her head. "Please, Miranda, if it wouldn't be too much trouble, will you bring Pauline's bed in here?"

"I guessed as much," Miranda said, moving Hilary's bed to one side.

"Hilary—wouldn't you truly rather have a room to yourself—for a change?" Pauline asked.

"I have had one to myself—for eight days —and, now I'm going back to the old way." Sitting among the cushions of the cozy corner, Hilary superintended operations, and when the two single white beds were standing side by side, in their accustomed fashion, the covers turned back for the night, she nodded in satisfied manner. "Thank you so much, Miranda; that's as it should be. Go get your things, Paul. To-morrow, you must move in regularly. Upper drawer between us, and the rest share and share alike, you know."

Patience, who had hit upon the happy

expedient of braiding her hair—braids, when
there were a lot of them, took a long time—
got slowly up from the hearth rug, her head
a sight to behold, with its tiny, hornlike
red braids sticking out in every direction. "I
suppose I'd better be going. I wish I had
someone to talk to, after I'd gone to bed."
And a deep sigh escaped her.

Pauline kissed the wistful little face.
"Never mind, old girl, you know you'd never
stay awake long enough to talk to anyone."

She and Hilary stayed awake talking, however, until Pauline's prudence got the better
of her joy in having her sister back in more
senses than one. It was so long since they
had had such a delightful bedtime talk.

"Seeing Winton First Club," Hilary said
musingly. "Paul, you're ever so clever.
Shirley insisted those letters stood for 'Sup-
pression of Woman's Foibles Club'; and Mr.
Dayre suggested they meant, 'Sweet Wild
Flowers.' "

"You've simply got to go to sleep now,
Hilary, else mother'll come and take me
away."

Hilary sighed blissfully. "I'll never say again—that nothing ever happens to us."

Tom and Josie came to supper the next night. Shirley was there, too, she had stopped in on her way to the post-office with her father that afternoon, to ask how Hilary was, and been captured and kept to supper and the first club meeting that followed.

Hilary had been sure she would like to join, and Shirley's prompt and delighted acceptance of their invitation proved her right.

"I've only got five names on my list," Tom said, as the young folks settled themselves on the porch after supper. "I suppose we'll think of others later."

"That'll make ten, counting us five, to begin with," Pauline said.

"Bell and Jack Ward," Tom took out his list, "the Dixon boys and Edna Ray. That's all."

"I'd just like to know where I come in, Tom Brice!" Patience demanded, her voice vibrant with indignation.

"Upon my word! I didn't suppose—"

"I am to belong!   Ain't I, Paul?"

"But Patty—"

"If you're going to say no, you needn't Patty me!"

"We'll see what mother thinks," Hilary suggested.   "You wouldn't want to be the only little girl to belong?"

"I shouldn't mind," Patience assured her, then feeling pretty sure that Pauline was getting ready to tell her to run away, she decided to retire on her own account.   That blissful time, when she should be "Miss Shaw," had one drawback, which never failed to assert itself at times like these—there would be no younger sister subject to her authority.

"Have you decided what we are to do?" Pauline asked Tom, when Patience had gone.

"I should say I had.   You'll be up to a ride by next Thursday, Hilary?   Not a very long ride."

"I'm sure I shall," Hilary answered eagerly.   "Where are we going?"

"That's telling."

"He won't even tell me," Josie said.

Tom's eyes twinkled.   "You're none of you

to know until next Thursday. Say, at four o'clock."

"Oh," Shirley said, "I think it's going to be the nicest club that ever was."

CHAPTER VI

"Am I late?" Shirley asked, as Pauline came down the steps to meet her Thursday afternoon.

"No, indeed, it still wants five minutes to four. Will you come in, or shall we wait out here? Hilary is under bond not to make her appearance until the last minute."

"Out here, please," Shirley answered, sitting down on the upper step. "What a delightful old garden this is. Father has at last succeeded in finding me my nag, horses appear to be at a premium in Winton, and even if he isn't first cousin to your Bedelia, I'm coming to take you and Hilary to drive some afternoon. Father got me a surrey, because, later, we're expecting some of the boys up, and we'll need a two-seated rig."

"We're coming to take you driving, too," Pauline said. "Just at present, it doesn't seem as if the summer would be long enough for all the things we mean to do in it."

"And you don't know yet, what we are to do this afternoon?"

"Only, that it's to be a drive and, after-wards, supper at the Brices'. That's all Josie, herself, knows about it. Tom had to take her and Mrs. Brice into so much of his confidence."

Through the drowsy stillness of the summer afternoon, came the notes of a horn, sounding nearer and nearer. A moment later, a stage drawn by two of the hotel horses turned in at the parsonage drive at a fine speed, drawing up before the steps where Pauline and Shirley were sitting, with considerable flourish. Beside the driver sat Tom, in long linen duster, the megaphone belonging to the school team in one hand. Along each side of the stage was a length of white cloth, on which was lettered—

SEEING WINTON STAGE

As the stage stopped, Tom sprang down, a most businesslike air on his boyish face.

"This is the Shaw residence, I believe?" he asked, consulting a piece of paper.

"I—I reckon so," Pauline answered, too taken aback to know quite what she was saying.

"All right!" Tom said. "I understand—"

"Then it's a good deal more than I do," Pauline cut in.

"That there are several young people here desirous of joining our little sight-seeing trip this afternoon."

From around the corner of the house at that moment peeped a small freckled face, the owner of which was decidedly very desirous of joining that trip. Only a deep sense of personal injury kept Patience from coming forward,—she wasn't going where she wasn't wanted—but some day—they'd see!

Shirley clapped her hands delightedly. "How perfectly jolly! Oh, I am glad you asked me to join the club."

"I'll go tell Hilary!" Pauline said. "Tom, how ever—"

"I beg your pardon, Miss?"

Pauline laughed and turned away.

"Oh, I say, Paul," Tom dropped his mask of pretended dignity, "let the Imp come with us—this time."

Pauline looked doubtful. She, as well as Tom, had caught sight of that small flushed face, on which longing and indignation had been so plainly written. "I'm not sure that mother will—" she began, "But I'll see."

"Tell her—just this first time," Tom urged, and Shirley added, "She would love it so."

"Mother says," Pauline reported presently, "that Patience may go *this* time—only we'll have to wait while she gets ready."

From an upper window came an eager voice. "I'm most ready now!"

"She'll never forget it—as long as she lives," Shirley said, "and if she hadn't gone she would never've forgotten *that*."

"Nor let us—for one while," Pauline remarked—"I'd a good deal rather work with than against that young lady."

Hilary came down then, looking ready and eager for the outing. She had been out in the trap with Pauline several times; once, even as far as the manor to call upon Shirley.

"Why," she exclaimed, "you've brought the Folly! Tom, how ever did you manage it?"

"Beg pardon, Miss?"

Hilary shrugged her shoulders, coming nearer for a closer inspection of the big lumbering stage. It had been new, when the present proprietor of the hotel, then a young man, now a middle-aged one, had come into his inheritance. Fresh back from a winter in town, he had indulged high hopes of booming his sleepy little village as a summer resort, and had ordered the stage—since christened the Folly—for the convenience and enjoyment of the guests—who had never come. A long idle lifetime the Folly had passed in the hotel carriage-house; used so seldom, as to make that using a village event, but never allowed to fall into disrepair, through some fancy of its owner.

As Tom opened the door at the back now, handing his guests in with much ceremony, Hilary laughed softly. "It doesn't seem quite—respectful to actually sit down in the poor old thing. I wonder, if it's more indignant, or pleased, at being dragged out into the light of day for a parcel of young folks?"

" 'Butchered to make a Roman Holiday'?" Shirley laughed.

At that moment Patience appeared, rather breathless—but not half as much so as Miranda, who had been drawn into service, and now appeared also—"You ain't half buttoned up behind, Patience!" she protested, "and your hair ribbon's not tied fit to be seen. —My sakes, to think of anyone ever having named that young one *Patience!*"

"I'll overhaul her, Miranda," Pauline comforted her. "Come here, Patience."

"Please, I am to sit up in front with you, ain't I, Tom?" Patience urged. "You and I always get on so beautifully together, you know."

Tom relaxed a second time. "I don't see how I can refuse after that," and the overhauling process being completed, Patience climbed up to the high front seat, where she beamed down on the rest with such a look of joyful content that they could only smile back in response.

From the doorway, came a warning voice. "Not too far, Tom, for Hilary; and remember, Patience, what you have promised me."

"All right, Mrs. Shaw," Tom assured her, and Patience nodded her head assentingly.

From the parsonage, they went first to the doctor's. Josie was waiting for them at the gate, and as they drew up before it, with horn blowing, and horses almost prancing—the proprietor of the hotel had given them his best horses, in honor of the Folly—she stared from her brother to the stage, with its white placard, with much the same look of wonder in her eyes as Pauline and Hilary had shown.

"Miss Brice?" Tom was consulting his list again.

"So that's what you've been concocting, Tom Brice!" Josie answered.

Tom's face was as sober as his manner. "I am afraid we are a little behind scheduled time, being unavoidably delayed."

"He means they had to wait for me to get ready," Patience explained. "You didn't expect to see me along, did you, Josie?" And she smiled blandly.

"I don't know what I did expect—certainly, not this." Josie took her place in the stage, not altogether sure whether the etiquette of the occasion allowed of her recognizing its other inmates, or not.

But Pauline nodded politely. "Good afternoon. Lovely day, isn't it?" she remarked, while Shirley asked, if she had ever made this trip before.

"Not in this way," Josie answered. "I've never ridden in the Folly before. Have you, Paul?"

"Once, from the depot to the hotel, when I was a youngster, about Impatience's age. You remember, Hilary?"

"Of course I do, Uncle Jerry took me up in front." Uncle Jerry was the name the owner of the stage went by in Winton. "He'd had a lot of Boston people up, and had been showing them around."

"This reminds me of the time father and I did our own New York in one of those big 'Seeing New York' motors," Shirley said. "I came home feeling almost as if we'd been making a trip 'round some foreign city."

"Tom can't make Winton seem foreign," Josie declared.

There were three more houses to stop at, lower down the street. From windows and porches all along the route, laughing, curious faces stared wonderingly after them, while a small body-guard of children sprang up as if by magic to attend them on their way. This added greatly to the delight of Patience, who smiled condescendingly down upon various intimates, blissfully conscious of the envy she was exciting in their breasts. It was delightful to be one of the club for a time, at least.

"And now, if you please, Ladies and Gentlemen," Tom had closed the door to upon the last of his party, "we will drive first to The Vermont House, a hostelry well known throughout the surrounding country, and conducted by one of Vermont's best known and honored sons."

"Hear! Hear!" Jack Ward cried. "I say, Tom, get that off again where Uncle Jerry can hear it, and you'll always be sure of his vote."

They had reached the rambling old hotel,

from the front porch of which Uncle Jerry himself, surveyed them genially.

"Ladies and Gentlemen," standing up, Tom turned to face the occupants of the stage, his megaphone, carried merely as a badge of office, raised like a conductor's baton, "I wish to impress upon your minds that the building now before you—liberal rates for the season —is chiefly remarkable for never having sheltered the Father of His Country."

"Now how do you know that?" Uncle Jerry protested. "Ain't that North Chamber called the 'Washington room'?"

"Oh, but that's because the first proprietor's first wife occupied that room—and she was famous for her Washington pie," Tom answered readily. "I assure you, sir, that any and all information which I shall have the honor to impart to these strangers within our gates may be relied upon for its accuracy." He gave the driver the word, and the Folly continued on its way, stopping presently before a little story-and-a-half cottage not far below the hotel and on a level with the street.

"This cottage, my young friends," Tom

said impressively, "should be—and I trust is —enshrined deep within the hearts of all true Wintonites. Latterly, it has come to be called the Barker cottage, but its real title is 'The Flag House'; so called, because from that humble porch, the first Stars and Stripes ever seen in Winton flung its colors to the breeze. The original flag is still in possession of a lineal descendant of its first owner, who is, unfortunately, not an inhabitant of this town." The boyish gravity of tone and manner was not all assumed now.

No one spoke for a moment; eleven pairs of young eyes were looking out at the little weather-stained building with new interest. "I thought," Bell Ward said at last, "that they called it the *flag* place, because someone of that name had used to live there."

"So did I," Hilary said.

As the stage moved on, Shirley leaned back for another look. "I shall get father to come and sketch it," she said. "Isn't it the quaintest old place?"

"We will now proceed," Tom announced, "to the village green, where I shall have the pleasure of relating to you certain anecdotes regarding the part it played in the early life of this interesting old village."

"Not too many, old man," Tracy Dixon suggested hurriedly, "or it may prove a one-sided pleasure."

The green lay in the center of the town,—a wide, open space, with flagstaff in the middle; fine old elms bordered it on all four sides. The Vermont House faced it, on the north, and on the opposite side stood the general store, belonging to Mr. Ward, with one or two smaller places of business.

"The business section" of the town, Tom called it, and quite failed to notice Tracy's lament that he had not brought his opera glasses with him. "Really, you know," Tracy explained to his companions, "I should have liked awfully to see it. I'm mighty interested in business sections."

"Cut that out," his brother Bob commanded, "the chap up in front is getting ready to hold forth again."

They were simple enough, those anecdotes, that "the chap up in front" told them; but in the telling, the boy's voice lost again all touch of mock gravity. His listeners, sitting there in the June sunshine, looking out across the old green, flecked with the waving tree shadows, and bright with the buttercups nodding here and there, seemed to see those men and boys drilling there in the far-off summer twilights; to hear the sharp words of command; the sound of fife and drum. And the familiar names mentioned more than once, well-known village names, names belonging to their own families in some instances, served to deepen the impression.

"Why," Edna Ray said slowly, "they're like the things one learns at school; somehow, they make one realize that there truly was a Revolutionary War. Wherever did you pick up such a lot of town history, Tom?"

"That's telling," Tom answered.

Back up the broad, main street they went, past the pleasant village houses, with their bright, well-kept dooryards, under the wide-spreading trees beneath which so many generations of young folks had come and gone; past the square, white parsonage, with its setting of green lawn; past the old stone church, and on out into the by-roads of the village, catching now and then a glimpse of the great lake beyond; and now and then, down some lane, a bit of the street they had left. They saw it all with eyes that for once had lost the indifference of long familiarity, and were swift to catch instead its quiet, restful beauty, helped in this, perhaps, by Shirley's very real admiration.

The ride ended at Dr. Brice's gate, and here Tom dropped his mantle of authority, handing all further responsibility as to the entertainment of the party over to his sister.

Hilary was carried off to rest until supper time, and the rest scattered about the garden, a veritable rose garden on that June afternoon, roses being Dr. Brice's pet hobby.

"It must be lovely to *live* in the country," Shirley said, dropping down on the grass before the doctor's favorite *La France,* and laying her face against the soft, pink petals of a half-blown bud.

Edna eyed her curiously. She had rather resented the admittance of this city girl into their set. Shirley's skirt and blouse were of white linen, there was a knot of red under the broad sailor collar, she was hatless and the dark hair,—never kept too closely within bounds—was tossed and blown; there was certainly nothing especially cityfied in either appearance or manner.

"That's the way *I* feel about the city," Edna said slowly, "it must be lovely to live *there.*"

Shirley laughed. "It is. I reckon just being alive anywhere such days as these ought to content one. You haven't been over to the manor lately, have you? I mean since we came there. We're really getting the garden to look like a garden. Reclaiming the wilderness, father calls it. You'll come over now, won't you—the club, I mean?"

"Why, of course," Edna answered, she thought she would like to go. "I suppose you've been over to the forts?"

"Lots of times—father's ever so interested in them, and it's just a pleasant row across, after supper."

"I have fasted too long, I must eat again,"

Tom remarked, coming across the lawn.
"Miss Dayre, may I have the honor?"

"Are you conductor, or merely club president now?" Shirley asked.

"Oh, I've dropped into private life again.
There comes Hilary—doesn't look much like
an invalid, does she?"

"But she didn't look very well the first time
I saw her," Shirley answered.

The long supper table was laid under the
apple trees at the foot of the garden, which in
itself served to turn the occasion into a festive
affair.

"You've given us a bully send-off, Mr.
President," Bob declared. "It's going to be
sort of hard for the rest of us to keep up with
you."

"By the way," Tom said, "Dr. Brice—some
of you may have heard of him—would like to
become an honorary member of this club.
Any contrary votes?"

"What's an honorary member?" Patience
asked. Patience had been remarkably good
that afternoon—so good that Pauline began to
feel worried, dreading the reaction.

"One who has all the fun and none of the work," Tracy explained, a merry twinkle in his brown eyes.

Patience considered the matter. "I shouldn't mind the work; but mother won't let me join regularly—mother takes notions now and then—but, please mayn't I be an honorary member?"

"Onery, you mean, young lady!" Tracy corrected.

Patience flashed a pair of scornful eyes at him. "Father says punning is the very lowest form of—"

"Never mind, Patience," Pauline said, "we haven't answered Tom yet. I vote we extend our thanks to the doctor for being willing to join."

"He isn't a bit more willing than I am," Patience observed. There was a general laugh among the real members, then Tom said, "If a Shaw votes for a Brice, I don't very well see how a Brice can refuse to vote for a Shaw."

"The motion is carried," Bob seconded him.

"Subject to mother's consent," Pauline

added, a quite unnecessary bit of elder sisterly interference, Patience thought.

"And now, even if it is telling on yourself, suppose you own up, old man?" Jack Ward turned to Tom. "You see we don't in the least credit you with having produced all that village history from your own stores of knowledge."

"I never said you need to," Tom answered, "even the idea was not altogether original with me."

Patience suddenly leaned forward, her face all alight with interest. "I love my love with an A," she said slowly, "because he's an— author."

Tom whistled. "Well, of all the uncanny young ones!"

"It's very simple," Patience said loftily.

"So it is, Imp," Tracy exclaimed; "I love him with an A, because he's an—A-M-E-R-I-C-A-N!"

"I took him to the sign of The Apple Tree," Bell took up the thread.

"And fed him (mentally) on subjects— antedeluvian, or almost so," Hilary added.

"What *are* you talking about?" Edna asked impatiently.

"Mr. Allen," Pauline told her.

"I saw him and Tom walking down the back lane the other night," Patience explained. Patience felt that she had won her right to belong to the club now—they'd see she wasn't just a silly little girl. "Father says he—I don't mean Tom—"

"We didn't suppose you did," Tracy laughed.

"Knows more history than any other man in the state; especially, the history of the state."

"Mr. Allen!" Shirley exclaimed. "T. C. Allen! Why, father and I read one of his books just the other week. It's mighty interesting. Does he live in Winton?"

"He surely does," Bob grinned, "and every little while he comes up to school and puts us through our paces. It's his boast that he was born, bred and educated right in Vermont. He isn't a bad old buck—if he wouldn't pester a fellow with too many questions."

"He lives out beyond us," Hilary told

Shirley. "There's a great apple tree right in front of the gate. He has an old house-keeper to look after him. I wish you could see his books—he's literally surrounded with them."

"Not storybooks," Patience added. "He says, they're books full of stories, if one's a mind to look for them."

"Please," Edna protested, "let's change the subject. Are we to have badges, or not?"

"Pins," Bell suggested.

"Pins would have to be made to order," Pauline objected, "and would be more or less expensive."

"And it's an unwritten by-law of this club, that we shall go to no unnecessary expense," Tom insisted.

"But—" Bell began.

"Oh, I know what you're thinking," Tom broke in, "but Uncle Jerry didn't charge for the stage—he said he was only too glad to have the poor thing used—'twas a dull life for her, shut up in the carriage-house year in and year out."

"The Folly isn't a she," Patience protested.

"Folly generally is feminine," Tracy said, "and so—"

"And he let us have the horses, too—for our initial outing," Tom went on. "Said the stage wouldn't be of much use without them."

"Three cheers for Uncle Jerry!" Bob Dixon cried. "Let's make him an honorary member."

"But the badges," Edna said. "I never saw such people for going off at tangents."

"Ribbon would be pretty," Shirley suggested, "with the name of the club in gilt letters. I can letter pretty well."

Her suggestion was received with general acclamation, and after much discussion, as to color, dark blue was decided on.

"Blue goes rather well with red," Tom said, "and as two of our members have red hair," his glance went from Patience to Pauline.

"I move we adjourn, the president's getting personal," Pauline pushed back her chair.

"Who's turn is it to be next?" Jack asked.

They drew lots with blades of grass; it fell to Hilary. "I warn you," she said, "that I can't come up to Tom."

Then the first meeting of the new club broke up, the members going their various ways. Shirley went as far as the parsonage, where she was to wait for her father.

"I've had a beautiful time," she said warmly. "And I've thought what to do when my turn comes. Only, I think you'll have to let father in as an honorary, I'll need him to help me out."

"We'll be only too glad," Pauline said heartily. "This club's growing fast, isn't it? Have you decided, Hilary?"

Hilary shook her head, "N-not exactly; I've sort of an idea."

CHAPTER VII

PAULINE and Hilary were up in their own room, the "new room," as it had come to be called, deep in the discussion of certain samples that had come in that morning's mail.

Uncle Paul's second check was due before long now, and then there were to be new summer dresses, or rather the goods for them, one apiece all around.

"Because, of course," Pauline said, turning the pretty scraps over, "Mother Shaw's got to have one, too. We'll have to get it—on the side—or she'll declare she doesn't need it, and she does."

"Just the goods won't come to so very much," Hilary said.

"No, indeed, and mother and I can make them."

"We certainly got a lot out of that other check, or rather, you and mother did," Hilary went on. "And it isn't all gone?"

"Pretty nearly, except the little we decided to lay by each month. But we did stretch it out in a good many directions. I don't suppose any of the other twenty-fives will seem quite so big."

"But there won't be such big things to get with them," Hilary said, "except these muslins."

"It's unspeakably delightful to have money for the little unnecessary things, isn't it?" Pauline rejoiced.

That first check had really gone a long ways. After buying the matting and paper, there had been quite a fair sum left; enough to pay for two magazine subscriptions, one a review that Mr. Shaw had long wanted to take, another, one of the best of the current monthlies; and to lay in quite a store of new ribbons and pretty turnovers, and several yards of silkaline to make cushion covers for the side porch, for Pauline, taking hint from Hilary's out-door parlor at the farm, had been quick to make the most of their own deep, vine-shaded side porch at the parsonage.

The front piazza belonged in a measure to the general public, there were too many people coming and going to make it private enough for a family gathering place. But the side porch was different, broad and square, only two or three steps from the ground; it was their favorite gathering place all through the long, hot summers.

With a strip of carpet for the floor, a small table resurrected from the garret, a bench and three wicker rockers, freshly painted green, and Hilary's hammock, rich in pillows, Pauline felt that their porch was one to be proud of. To Patience had been entrusted the care of keeping the old blue and white canton bowl filled with fresh flowers, and there were generally books and papers on the table. And they might have done it all before, Pauline thought now, if they had stopped to think.

"Have you decided?" Hilary asked her, glancing at the sober face bent over the samples.

"I believe I'd forgotten all about them; I

think I'll choose this—" Pauline held up a sample of blue and white striped dimity.

"That *is* pretty."

"You can have it, if you like."

"Oh, no, I'll have the pink."

"And the lavender dot, for Mother Shaw?"

"Yes," Hilary agreed.

"Patience had better have straight white, it'll be in the wash so often."

"Why not let her choose for herself, Paul?" Hilary suggested.

"Hilary! Oh, Hilary Shaw!" Patience called excitedly, at that moment from downstairs.

"Up here!" Hilary called back, and Patience came hurrying up, stumbling more than once in her eagerness. The next moment, she pushed wide the door of the "new room." "See what's come! It's addressed to you, Hilary—it came by express—Jed brought it up from the depot!" Jed was the village expressman.

She deposited her burden on the table beside Hilary. It was a good-sized, square box, and with all that delightful air of mystery about it that such packages usually have.

"What do you suppose it is, Paul?" Hilary cried. "Why, I've never had anything come unexpectedly, like this, before."

"A whole lot of things are happening to us that never've happened before," Patience said. "See, it's from Uncle Paul!" she pointed to the address at the upper left-hand corner of the package. "Oh, Hilary, let *me* open it, please, I'll go get the tack hammer."

"Tell mother to come," Hilary said.

"Maybe it's books, Paul!" she added, as Patience scampered off.

Pauline lifted the box. "It doesn't seem quite heavy enough for books."

"But what else could it be?"

Pauline laughed. "It isn't another Bedelia, at all events. It could be almost anything. Hilary, I believe Uncle Paul is really glad I wrote to him."

"Well, I'm not exactly sorry," Hilary declared.

"Mother can't come yet," Patience explained, reappearing. "She says not to wait.

It's that tiresome Mrs. Dane; she just seems to know when we don't want her, and then to come—only, I suppose if she waited 'til we did want to see her, she'd never get here."

"Mother didn't say that, Impatience, and you'd better not let her hear you saying it," Pauline warned.

But Patience was busy with the tack hammer. "You can take the inside covers off," she said to Hilary.

"Thanks, awfully," Hilary murmured.

"It'll be my turn next, won't it?" Patience dropped the tack hammer, and wrenched off the cover of the box—"Go ahead, Hilary! Oh, how slow you are!"

For Hilary was going about her share of the unpacking in the most leisurely way. "I want to guess first," she said. "Such a lot of wrappings! It must be something breakable."

"A picture, maybe," Pauline suggested. Patience dropped cross-legged on the floor. "Then *I* don't think Uncle Paul's such a very sensible sort of person," she said.

"No, not pictures!" Hilary lifted something from within the box, "but something to get pictures with. See, Paul!"

"A camera! Oh, Hilary!"

"And not a little tiny one." Patience leaned over to examine the box. "It's a three and a quarter by four and a quarter. We can have fun now, can't we?" Patience believed firmly in the coöperative principle.

"Tom'll show you how to use it," Pauline said. "He fixed up a dark room last fall, you know, for himself."

"And here are all the doings." Patience came to investigate the further contents of the express package. "Films and those funny little pans for developing in, and all."

Inside the camera was a message to the effect that Mr. Shaw hoped his niece would be pleased with his present and that it would add to the summer's pleasures.

"He's getting real uncley, isn't he?" Patience observed. Then she caught sight of the samples Pauline had let fall. "Oh, how pretty! Are they for dresses for us?"

"They'd make pretty scant ones, I'd say," Pauline answered.

"Silly!" Patience spread the bright scraps out on her blue checked gingham apron. "I just bet you've been choosing! Why didn't you call me?"

"To help us choose?" Pauline asked, with a laugh.

But at the present moment, her small sister was quite impervious to sarcasm. "I think I'll have this," she pointed to a white ground, closely sprinkled with vivid green dots.

"Carrots and greens!" Pauline declared, glancing at her sister's red curls. "You'd look like an animated boiled dinner! If you please, who said anything about your choosing?"

"You look ever so nice in all white, Patty," Hilary said hastily.

"Have you and Paul chosen all white?"

"N-no."

"Then I shan't!" She looked up quickly, her blue eyes very persuasive. "I don't very often have a brand new, just-out-of-the-store dress, do I?"

Pauline laughed. "Only don't let it be the green then. Good, here's mother, at last!"

"Mummy, is blue or green better?" Patience demanded.

Mrs. Shaw examined and duly admired the camera, and decided in favor of a blue dot; then she said, "Mrs. Boyd is down-stairs, Hilary."

"How nice!" Hilary jumped up. "I want to see her most particularly."

"Bless me, child!" Mrs. Boyd exclaimed, as Hilary came into the sitting-room, "how you are getting on! Why, you don't look like the same girl of three weeks back."

Hilary sat down beside her on the sofa. "I've got a most tremendous favor to ask, Mrs. Boyd."

"I'm glad to hear that! I hear you young folks are having fine times lately. Shirley was telling me about the club the other night."

"It's about the club—and it's in two parts; first, won't you and Mr. Boyd be honorary members?—That means you can come to the good times if you like, you know.—And the other is—you see, it's my turn next—" And when Pauline came down, she found the two deep in consultation.

The next afternoon, Patience carried out her long-intended plan of calling at the manor. Mrs. Shaw was from home for the day, Pauline and Hilary were out in the trap with Tom and Josie and the camera. "So there's really no one to ask permission of, Towser," Patience explained, as they started off down the back lane. "Father's got the study door *closed,* of course that means he mustn't be disturbed for anything unless it's absolutely necessary."

Towser wagged comprehendingly. He was quite ready for a ramble this bright afternoon, especially a ramble 'cross lots.

Shirley and her father were not at home, neither—which was even more disappointing —were any of the dogs; so, after a short chat with Betsy Todd, considerably curtailed by that body's too frankly expressed wonder that Patience should've been allowed to come unattended by any of her elders, she and Towser wandered home again.

In the lane, they met Sextoness Jane, sitting on the roadside, under a shady tree. She and Patience exchanged views on parish matters, discussed the new club, and had an all-round good gossip.

"My sakes!" Jane said, her faded eyes bright with interest, "it must seem like Christmas all the time up to your house." She looked past Patience to the old church beyond, around which her life had centered itself for so many years. "There weren't ever such doings at the parsonage—nor anywhere else, what I knowed of—when I was a girl. Why, that Bedelia horse! Seems like she give an air to the whole place—so pretty and high-stepping—it's most's good's a circus—not that I've ever been to a circus, but I've hear tell on them—just to see her go prancing by."

"I think," Patience said that evening, as they were all sitting on the porch in the twilight, "I think that Jane would like awfully to belong to our club."

"Have you started a club, too?" Pauline teased.

Patience tossed her red head. "'The S. W. F. Club,' I mean; and you know it, Paul Shaw. When I get to be fifteen, I shan't act half so silly as some folks."

"What ever put that idea in your head?" Hilary asked. It was one of Hilary's chief missions in life to act as intermediary between her younger and older sister.

"Oh, I just gathered it, from what she said. Towser and I met her this afternoon, on our way home from the manor."

"From where, Patience?" her mother asked quickly, with that faculty for taking hold of the wrong end of a remark, that Patience had had occasion to deplore more than once.

And in the diversion this caused, Sextoness Jane was forgotten.

"Here comes Mr. Boyd, Hilary!" Pauline called from the foot of the stairs.

Hilary finished tying the knot of cherry ribbon at her throat, then snatching up her big sun-hat from the bed, she ran down-stairs.

Before the side door, stood the big wagon, in which Mr. Boyd had driven over from the farm, its bottom well filled with fresh straw. For Hilary's outing was to be a cherry picnic at The Maples, with supper under the trees, and a drive home later by moonlight.

Shirley had brought over the badges a day
or two before; the blue ribbon, with its gilt
lettering, gave an added touch to the girls'
white dresses and cherry ribbons.

Mr. Dayre had been duly made an honorary
member. He and Shirley were to meet the
rest of the party at the farm. As for
Patience H. M., as Tom called her, she had
been walking very softly the past few days.
There had been no long rambles without permission, no making calls on her own account.
There *had* been a private interview between
herself and Mr. Boyd, whom she had met, not
altogether by chance, down street the day before.

The result was that, at the present moment,
Patience—white-frocked, blue-badged, cher-
ry-ribboned—was sitting demurely in one
corner of the big wagon.

Mr. Boyd chuckled as he glanced down at
her; a body'd have to get up pretty early in
the morning to get ahead of that youngster.
Though not in white, nor wearing cherry
ribbons, Mr. Boyd sported his badge with
much complacency. Winton was looking up,

decidedly. 'Twasn't such a slow old place,
after all.

"All ready?" he asked, as Pauline slipped a
couple of big pasteboard boxes under the
wagon seat, and threw in some shawls for the
coming home.

"All ready. Good-by, Mother Shaw. Remember, you and father have got to come
with us one of these days. I guess if Mr.
Boyd can take a holiday you can."

"Good-by," Hilary called, and Patience
waved joyously. "This'll make two times,"
she comforted herself, "and two times ought
to be enough to establish what father calls 'a
precedent.'"

They stopped at the four other houses in
turn; then Mr. Boyd touched his horses up
lightly, rattling them along at a good rate cut
on to the road leading to the lake and so to
The Maples.

There was plenty of fun and laughter by
the way. They had gone picnicking together
so many summers, this same crowd, had had so
many good times together. "And yet it seems
different, this year, doesn't it?" Bell said.

"We really aren't doing new things—exactly, still they seem so."

Tracy touched his badge. "These are the 'Blue Ribbon Brand,' best goods in the market."

"Come to think of it, there aren't so very many new things one can do," Tom remarked.

"Not in Winton, at any rate," Bob added.

"If anyone dares say anything derogatory to Winton, on this, or any other, outing of the 'S. W. F. Club,' he, or she, will get into trouble," Josie said sternly.

Mrs. Boyd was waiting for them on the steps, Shirley close by, while a glimpse of a white umbrella seen through the trees told that Mr. Dayre was not far off.

"It's the best cherry season in years," Mrs. Boyd declared, as the young folks came laughing and crowding about her. She was a prime favorite with them all. "My, how nice you look! Those badges are mighty pretty."

"Where's yours?" Pauline demanded.

"It's in my top drawer, dear. Looks like I'm too old to go wearing such things, though 'twas ever so good in you to send me one."

"Hilary," Pauline turned to her sister, "I'm sure Mrs. Boyd'll let you go to her top drawer. Not a stroke of business does this club do, until this particular member has her badge on."

"Now," Tom asked, when that little matter had been attended to, "what's the order of the day?"

"I hope you've worn old dresses?" Mrs. Boyd said.

"I haven't, ma'am," Tracy announced.

"Order!" Bob called.

"Eat all you like—so long's you don't get sick—and each pick a nice basket to take home," Mrs. Boyd explained. There were no cherries anywhere else quite so big and fine, as those at The Maples.

"You to command, we to obey!" Tracy declared.

"Boys to pick, girls to pick up," Tom ordered, as they scattered about among the big, bountifully laden trees.

"For cherry time,
    Is merry time,"

Shirley improvised, catching the cluster of great red and white cherries Jack tossed down to her.

Even more than the rest of the young folks, Shirley was getting the good of this happy, out-door summer, with its quiet pleasures and restful sense of home life. She had never known anything before like it. It was very different, certainly, from the studio life in New York, different from the sketching rambles she had taken other summers with her father. They were delightful, too, and it was pleasant to think of going back to them again —some day; but just at present, it was good to be a girl among other girls, interested in all the simple, homely things each day brought up.

And her father was content, too, else how could she have been so? It was doing him no end of good. Painting a little, sketching a little, reading and idling a good deal, and through it all, immensely amused at the enthusiasm with which his daughter threw herself into the village life. "I shall begin to think soon, that you were born and raised in

Winton," he had said to her that very morning, as she came in fresh from a conference
with Betsy Todd. Betsy might be spending
her summer in a rather out-of-the-way spot,
and her rheumatism might prevent her from
getting into town—as she expressed it—but
very little went on that Betsy did not hear of,
and she was not one to keep her news to herself.

"So shall I," Shirley had laughed back.
She wondered now, if Pauline or Hilary
would enjoy a studio winter, as much as she
was reveling in her Winton summer? She
decided that probably they would.

Cherry time *was* merry time that afternoon.
Of course, Bob fell out of one of the trees, but
Bob was so used to tumbling, and the others
were so used to having him tumble, that no
one paid much attention to it; and equally, of
course, Patience tore her dress and had to be
taken in hand by Mrs. Boyd.

"Every rose must have its thorns, you know,
kid," Tracy told her, as she was borne away
for this enforced retirement. "We'll leave a
few cherries, 'gainst you get back."

Patience elevated her small freckled nose, she was an adept at it. "I reckon they will be mighty few—if you have anything to do with it."

"You're having a fine time, aren't you, Senior?" Shirley asked, as Mr. Dayre came scrambling down from his tree; he had been routed from his sketching and pressed into service by his indefatigable daughter.

"Scrumptious! Shirley, you've got a fine color—only it's laid on in spots."

"You're spattery, too," she retorted. "I must go help lay out the supper now."

"Will anyone want supper, after so many cherries?" Mr. Dayre asked.

"Will they?" Pauline laughed. "Well, you just wait and see."

Some of the boys brought the table from the house, stretching it out to its uttermost length. The girls laid the cloth, Mrs. Boyd provided, and unpacked the boxes stacked on the porch. From the kitchen came an appetizing odor of hot coffee. Hilary and Bell went off after flowers for the center of the table.

"We'll put one at each place, suggestive of the person—like a place card," Hilary proposed.

"Here's a daisy for Mrs. Boyd," Bell laughed.

"Let's give that to Mr. Boyd and cut her one of these old-fashioned spice pinks," Hilary said.

"Better put a bit of pepper-grass for the Imp," Tracy suggested, as the girls went from place to place up and down the long table.

"Paul's to have a pansy," Hilary insisted. She remembered how, if it hadn't been for Pauline's "thought" that wet May afternoon, everything would still be as dull and dreary as it was then.

At her own place she found a spray of belated wild roses, Tom had laid there, the pink of their petals not more delicate than the soft color coming and going in the girl's face.

"We've brought for-get-me-not for you, Shirley," Bell said, "so that you won't forget us when you get back to the city."

"As if I were likely to!" Shirley exclaimed.

"Sound the call to supper, sonny!" Tom told

Bob, and Bob, raising the farm dinner-horn, sounded it with a will, making the girls cover their ears with their hands and bringing the boys up with a rush.

"It's a beautiful picnic, isn't it?" Patience said, reappearing in time to slip into place with the rest.

"And after supper, I will read you the club song," Tracy announced.

"Are we to have a club song?" Edna asked.

"We are."

"Read it now, son—while we eat," Tom suggested.

Tracy rose promptly—"Mind you save me a few scraps then. First, it isn't original—"

"All the better," Jack commented.

"Hush up, and listen —

    " 'A cheerful world?—It surely is.
      And if you understand your biz
      You'll taboo the worry worm,
      And cultivate the happy germ.

    " 'It's a habit to be happy,
      Just as much as to be scrappy.
      So put the frown away awhile,
      And try a little sunny smile.' "

There was a generous round of applause. Tracy tossed the scrap of paper across the table to Bell. "Put it to music, before the next round-up, if you please."

Bell nodded. "I'll do my best."

"We've got a club song and a club badge, and we ought to have a club motto," Josie said.

"It's right to your hand, in your song," her brother answered. " 'It's a habit to be happy.' "

"Good!" Pauline seconded him, and the motto was at once adopted.

CHAPTER VIII

BELL WARD set the new song to music, a light, catchy tune, easy to pick up. It took immediately, the boys whistled it, as they came and went, and the girls hummed it. Patience, with cheerful impartiality, did both, in season and out of season.

It certainly looked as though it were getting to be a habit to be happy among a good many persons in Winton that summer. The spirit of the new club seemed in the very atmosphere.

A rivalry, keen but generous, sprang up between the club members in the matter of discovering new ways of "Seeing Winton," or, failing that, of giving a new touch to the old familiar ones.

There were many informal and unexpected outings, besides the club's regular ones, sometimes amongst all the members, often among two or three of them.

Frequently, Shirley drove over in the surrey, and she and Pauline and Hilary, with sometimes one of the other girls, would go for long rambling drives along the quiet country roads, or out beside the lake. Shirley generally brought her sketch-book and there were pleasant stoppings here and there.

And there were few days on which Bedelia and the trap were not out, Bedelia enjoying the brisk trots about the country quite as much as her companions.

Hilary soon earned the title of "the kodak fiend," Josie declaring she took pictures in her sleep, and that "Have me; have my camera," was Hilary's present motto. Certainly, the camera was in evidence at all the outings, and so far, Hilary had fewer failures to her account than most beginners. Her "picture diary" she called the big scrap-book in which was mounted her record of the summer's doings.

Those doings were proving both numerous and delightful. Mr. Shaw, as an honorary

member, had invited the club to a fishing
party, which had been an immense success.
The doctor had followed it by a moonlight
drive along the lake and across on the old sail
ferry to the New York side, keeping strictly
within that ten-mile-from-home limit, though
covering considerably more than ten miles in
the coming and going.

There had been picnics of every description,
to all the points of interest and charm in and
about the village; an old-time supper at the
Wards', at which the club members had appeared in old-fashioned costumes; a straw-
berry supper on the church lawn, to which all
the church were invited, and which went off
rather better than some of the sociables had in
times past.

As the Winton *Weekly News* declared
proudly, it was the gayest summer the village
had known in years. Mr. Paul Shaw's theory
about developing home resources was proving
a sound one in this instance at least.

Hilary had long since forgotten that she
had ever been an invalid, had indeed, sometimes, to be reminded of that fact. She had

quite discarded the little "company" fiction, except now and then, by way of a joke. "Who'd want to be company?" she protested. "I'd rather be one of the family these days."

"That's all very well," Patience retorted, "when you're getting all the good of being both. You've got the company room." Patience had not found her summer quite as cloudless as some of her elders; being an honorary member had not meant *all* of the fun in her case. She wished very much that it were possible to grow up in a single night, thus wiping out forever that drawback of being "a little girl."

Still, on the whole, she managed to get a fair share of the fun going on and quite agreed with the editor of the *Weekly News,* going so far as to tell him so when she met him down street. She had a very kindly feeling in her heart for the pleasant spoken little editor; had he not given her her full honors every time she had had the joy of being "among those present"?

There had been three of those checks from Uncle Paul; it was wonderful how far each

had been made to go. It was possible nowadays to send for a new book, when the reviews
were more than especially tempting. There
had also been a tea-table added to the other
attractions of the side porch, not an expensive
affair, but the little Japanese cups and
saucers were both pretty and delicate, as was
the rest of the service; while Miranda's cream
cookies and sponge cakes were, as Shirley declared, good enough to be framed. Even the
minister appeared now and then of an afternoon, during tea hour, and the young people,
gathered on the porch, began to find him a
very pleasant addition to their little company,
he and they getting acquainted, as they had
never gotten acquainted before.

Sextoness Jane came every week now to
help with the ironing, which meant greater
freedom in the matter of wash dresses; and
also, to Sextoness Jane herself, the certainty
of a day's outing every week. To Sextoness
Jane, those Tuesdays at the parsonage were
little short of a dissipation. Miranda, un-
bending in the face of such sincere and humble
admiration, was truly gracious. The glimpses

the little bent, old sextoness got of the young
folks, the sense of life going on about her, were
as good as a play, to quote her own simile,
confided of an evening to Tobias, her great
black cat, the only other inmate of the old cottage.

"I reckon Uncle Paul would be rather surprised," Pauline said one evening, "if he could
know all the queer sorts of ways in which we
use his money. But the little easings-up do
count for so much."

"Indeed they do," Hilary agreed warmly,
"though it hasn't all gone for easings-ups, as
you call them, either." She had sat down
right in the middle of getting ready for bed,
to revel in her ribbon box; she so loved pretty
ribbons!

The committee on finances, as Pauline
called her mother, Hilary, and herself, held
frequent meetings. "And there's always one
thing," the girl would declare proudly, "the
treasury is never entirely empty."

She kept faithful account of all money received and spent; each month a certain amount
was laid away for the "rainy day"—which

meant, really, the time when the checks should cease to come—"for, you know, Uncle Paul only promised them for the *summer*," Pauline reminded the others, and herself, rather frequently. Nor was all of the remainder ever quite used up before the coming of the next check.

"You're quite a business woman, my dear," Mr. Shaw said once, smiling over the carefully recorded entries in the little account-book she showed him. "We must have named you rightly."

She wrote regularly to her uncle; her letters unconsciously growing more friendly and informal from week to week. They were bright, vivid letters, more so than Pauline had any idea of. Through them, Mr. Paul Shaw felt himself becoming very well acquainted with these young relatives whom he had never seen, and in whom, as the weeks went by, he felt himself growing more and more interested.

Without realizing it, he got into the habit of looking forward to that weekly letter; the girl wrote a nice clear hand, there didn't seem

to be any nonsense about her, and she had a
way of going right to her point that was most
satisfactory. It seemed sometimes as if he
could see the old white parsonage and ivy-
covered church; the broad tree-shaded lawns;
the outdoor parlor, with the young people
gathered about the tea-table; Bedelia, picking her way along the quiet country roads;
the great lake in all its moods; the manor
house.

Sometimes Pauline would enclose one or
two of Hilary's snap-shots of places, or persons. At one of these, taken the day of the
fishing picnic, and under which Hilary had
written "The best catch of the season," Mr.
Paul Shaw looked long and intently. Somehow he had never pictured Phil to himself as
middle-aged. If anyone had told him, when
the lad was a boy, that the time would come
when they would be like strangers to each
other—Mr. Paul Shaw slipped the snap-shot
and letter back into their envelope.

It was that afternoon that he spent considerable time over a catalogue devoted entirely to sporting goods; and it was a fort-

night later that Patience came flying down the garden path to where Pauline and Hilary were leaning over the fence, paying a morning call to Bedelia, sunning herself in the back pasture.

"You'll *never* guess what's come *this* time! And Jed says he reckons he can haul it out this afternoon if you're set on it! And it's addressed to the 'Misses Shaw,' so that means it's *mine, too!*" Patience dropped on the grass, quite out of breath.

The "it" proved to be a row-boat with a double set of oar-locks, a perfect boat for the lake, strong and safe, but trig and neat of outline.

Hilary named it the "Surprise" at first sight, and Tom was sent for at once to paint the name in red letters to look well against the white background and to match the boat's red trimmings.

Its launching was an event. Some of the young people had boats over at the lake, rather weather-beaten, tubby affairs, Bell declared them, after the coming of the "Surprise." A general overhauling took place immediately, the girls adopted simple boating dresses—red and white, which were their boating colors. A new zest was given to the water picnics, Bedelia learning to know the lake road very well.

August had come before they fairly realized that their summer was more than well under way. In little more than a month the long vacation would be over. Tom and Josie were to go to Boston to school; Bell to Vergennes.

"There'll never be another summer quite like it!" Hilary said one morning. "I can't bear to think of its being over."

"It isn't—yet," Pauline answered.

"Tom's coming," Patience heralded from the gate, and Hilary ran indoors for hat and camera.

"Where are you off to this morning?" Pauline asked, as her sister came out again.

"Out by the Cross-roads' Meeting-House," Tom answered. "Hilary has designs on it, I believe."

"You'd better come, too, Paul," Hilary urged. "It's a glorious morning for a walk."

"I'm going to help mother cut out; perhaps

I'll come to meet you with Bedelia 'long towards noon. You wait at Meeting-House Hill."

"*I'm* not going to be busy this morning," Patience insinuated.

"Oh, yes you are, young lady," Pauline told her. "Mother said you were to weed the aster bed."

Patience looked longingly after the two starting gayly off down the path, their cameras swung over their shoulders, then she looked disgustedly at the aster bed. It was quite the biggest of the smaller beds.—She didn't see what people wanted to plant so many asters for; she had never cared much for asters, she felt she should care even less about them in the future. Tiresome, stiff affairs!

By the time Tom and Hilary reached the old Cross-Roads' Meeting-House that morning, after a long roundabout ramble, Hilary, for one, was quite willing to sit down and wait for Pauline and the trap, and eat the great, juicy blackberries Tom gathered for her from the bushes along the road.

It had rained during the night and the air

was crisp and fresh, with a hint of the coming
fall. "Summer's surely on the down grade,"
Tom said, throwing himself on the bank beside Hilary.

"So Paul and I were lamenting this morning. I don't suppose it matters as much to
you folks who are going off to school."

"Still it means another summer over," Tom
said soberly. He was rather sorry that it
was so—there could never be another summer
quite so jolly and carefree. "And the breaking up of the club, I suppose?"

"I don't see why we need call it a break—
just a discontinuance, for a time."

"And why that, even? There'll be a lot
of you left, to keep it going."

"Y-yes, but with three, or perhaps more,
out, I reckon we'll have to postpone the next
installment until another summer."

Tom went off then for more berries, and
Hilary sat leaning back against the trunk of
the big tree crowning the top of Meeting-
House Hill, her eyes rather thoughtful.
From where she sat, she had a full view of both
roads for some distance and, just beyond, the

little hamlet scattered about the old meeting-house.

Before the gate of one of the houses stood a familiar gig, and presently, as she sat watching, Dr. Brice came down the narrow flower-bordered path, followed by a woman. At the gate both stopped; the woman was saying something, her anxious, drawn face seeming out of keeping with the cheery freshness of the morning and the flowers nodding their bright heads about her.

As the doctor stood listening, his old shabby medicine case in his hand, with face bent to the troubled one raised to his, and bearing indicating grave sympathy and understanding, Hilary reached for her camera.

"Upon my word! Isn't the poor pater exempt?" Tom laughed, coming back.

"I want it for the book Josie and I are making for you to take away with you, 'Winton Snap-shots.' We'll call it 'The Country Doctor.' "

Tom looked at the gig, moving slowly off down the road now. He hated to say so, but he wished Hilary would not put that particular snap-shot in. He had a foreboding that it was going to make him a bit uncomfortable —later—when the time for decision came; though, as for that, he had already decided— beyond thought of change. He wished that the pater hadn't set his heart on his coming back here to practice—and he wished, too, that Hilary hadn't taken that photo.

"Paul's late," he said presently.

"I'm afraid she isn't coming."

"It's past twelve," Tom glanced at the sun. "Maybe we'd better walk on a bit."

But they had walked a considerable bit, all the way to the parsonage, in fact, before they saw anything of Pauline. There, she met them at the gate. "Have you seen any trace of Patience—and Bedelia?" she asked eagerly.

"Patience and Bedelia?" Hilary repeated wonderingly.

"They're both missing, and it's pretty safe guessing they're together."

"But Patience would never dare—"

"Wouldn't she!" Pauline exclaimed. "Jim brought Bedelia 'round about eleven and when I came out a few moments later, she was gone and so was Patience. Jim's out looking for them. We traced them as far as the Lake road."

"I'll go hunt, too," Tom offered. "Don't you worry, Paul; she'll turn up all right—couldn't down the Imp, if you tried."

"But she's never driven Bedelia alone; and Bedelia's not Fanny."

However, half an hour later, Patience drove calmly into the yard, Towser on the seat beside her, and if there was something very like anxiety in her glance, there was distinct triumph in the way she carried her small, bare head.

"We've had a beautiful drive!" she announced, smiling pleasantly from her high seat, at the worried, indignant group on the porch. "I tell you, there isn't any need to 'hi-yi' this horse!"

"My sakes!" Miranda declared. "Did you ever hear the beat of that!"

"Get down, Patience!" Mrs. Shaw said, and Patience climbed obediently down. She bore the prompt banishment to her own room which followed, with seeming indifference.

Certainly, it was not unexpected; but when Hilary brought her dinner up to her presently, she found her sitting on the floor, her head on the bed. It was only a few days now to Shirley's turn and it was going to be such a nice turn. Patience felt that for once Patience Shaw had certainly acted most unwisely.

"Patty, how could you!" Hilary put the tray on the table and sitting down on the bed, took the tumbled head on her knee. "We've been so worried! You see, Bedelia isn't like Fanny!"

"That's why I wanted to get a chance to drive her by myself for once! She went beautifully! out on the Lake road I just let her loose!" For the moment, pride in her recent performance routed all contrition from Patience's voice—"I tell you, folks I passed just stared!"

"Patience, how—"

"I wasn't scared the least bit; and, of course, Bedelia knew it. Uncle Jerry says they always know when you're scared, and if Mr. Allen is the most up in history of any

man in Vermont, Uncle Jerry is the most in
horses."

Hilary felt that the conversation was hardly
proceeding upon the lines her mother would
have approved of, especially under present
circumstances. "That has nothing to do with
it, you know, Patience," she said, striving to
be properly severe.

"I think it has—everything. I think it's
nice not being scared of things. You're sort
of timid 'bout things, aren't you, Hilary?"

Hilary made a movement to rise.

"Oh, please," Patience begged. "It's going to be such a dreadful long afternoon—all
alone."

"But I can't stay, mother would not
want—"

"Just for a minute. I—I want to tell you
something. I—coming back, I met Jane,
and I gave her a lift home—and she did love
it so—she says she's never ridden before behind a horse that really went as if it enjoyed
it as much as she did. That was some good
out of being bad, wasn't it? And—I told you
—ever'n' ever so long ago, that I was mighty

sure Jane'd just be tickled to death to belong
to our club. I think you might ask her—I
don't see why she shouldn't like Seeing Winton, same's we do—she doesn't ever have fun
—and she'll be dead pretty soon. She's getting along, Jane is—it'd make me mad's anything to have to die 'fore I'd had any fun to
speak of. Jane's really very good company
—when you draw her out—she just needs
drawing out—Jane does. Seems to me, she
remembers every funeral and wedding and
everything—that's ever taken place in Winton." Patience stopped, sheer out of breath,
but there was an oddly serious look on her little eager face.

Hilary stroked back the tangled red curls.
"Maybe you're right, Patty; maybe we have
been selfish with our good times. I'll have to
go now, dear. You—I may tell mother—
that you *are* sorry—truly, Patty?"

Patience nodded. "But I reckon, it's a
good deal on account of Shirley's turn," she
explained.

Hilary bit her lip.

"You don't suppose you could fix that up

with mother? You're pretty good at fixing things up with mother, Hilary."

"Since how long?" Hilary laughed, but when she had closed the door, she opened it again to stick her head in. "I'll try, Patty, at any rate," she promised.

She went down-stairs rather thoughtful. Mrs. Shaw was busy in the study and Pauline had gone out on an errand. Hilary went up-stairs again, going to sit by one of the side windows in the "new room."

Over at the church, Sextoness Jane was making ready for the regular weekly prayer meeting; never a service was held in the church that she did not set all in order. Through one of the open windows, Hilary caught sight of the bunch of flowers on the reading-desk. Jane had brought them with her from home. Presently, the old woman herself came to the window to shake her dust-cloth, standing there a moment, leaning a little out, her eyes turned to the parsonage. Pauline was coming up the path, Shirley and Bell were with her. They were laughing and talking, the bright young voices making a pleasant break in the quiet of the garden. It seemed to Hilary, as if she could catch the wistful look in Jane's faded eyes, a look only half consciously so, as if the old woman reached out vaguely for something that her own youth had been without and that only lately she had come to feel the lack of.

A quick lump came into the girl's throat. Life had seemed so bright and full of untried possibilities only that very morning, up there on Meeting-House Hill, with the wind in one's face; and then had come that woman, following the doctor down from the path. Life was surely anything but bright for her this crisp August day—and now here was Jane. And presently—at the moment it seemed very near indeed to Hilary—she and Paul and all of them would be old and, perhaps, unhappy. And then it would be good to remember—that they had tried to share the fun and laughter of this summer of theirs with others.

Hilary thought of the piece of old tapestry hanging on the studio wall over at the manor —of the interwoven threads—the dark as necessary to the pattern as the bright. Perhaps they had need of Sextoness Jane, of the interweaving of her life into theirs—of the interweaving of all the village lives going on about them—quite as much as those more sober lives needed the brightening touch of theirs.

"Hilary! O Hilary!" Pauline called.

"I'm coming," Hilary answered, and went slowly down to where the others were waiting on the porch.

"Has anything happened?" Pauline asked.

"I've been having a think—and I've come to the conclusion that we're a selfish, self-absorbed set."

"Mother Shaw!" Pauline went to the study window, "please come out here. Hilary's calling us names, and that isn't polite."

Mrs. Shaw came. "I hope not very bad names," she said.

Hilary swung slowly back and forth in the hammock. "I didn't mean it that way—it's only—" She told what Patience had said about Jane's joining the club, and then, rather reluctantly, a little of what she had been thinking.

"I think Hilary's right," Shirley declared. "Let's form a deputation and go right over and ask the poor old soul to join here and now."

"I would never've thought of it," Bell said. "But I don't suppose I've ever given Jane a thought, anyway."

"Patty's mighty cute—for all she's such a terror at times," Pauline admitted. "She knows a lot about the people here—and it's just because she's interested in them."

"Come on," Shirley said, jumping up. "We're going to have another honorary member."

"I think it would be kind, girls," Mrs. Shaw said gravely. "Jane will feel herself immensely flattered, and I know of no one who upholds the honor of Winton more honestly or persistently."

"And please, Mrs. Shaw," Shirley coaxed, "when we come back, mayn't Patience Shaw, H. M., come down and have tea with us?"

"I hardly think—"

"Please, Mother Shaw," Hilary broke in; "after all—she started this, you know. That sort of counterbalances the other, doesn't it?"

"Well, we'll see," her mother laughed.

Pauline ran to get one of the extra badges with which Shirley had provided her, and then the four girls went across to the church.

Sextoness Jane was just locking the back door—not the least important part of the afternoon's duties with her—as they came through the opening in the hedge. "Good afternoon," she said cheerily, "was you wanting to go inside?"

"No," Pauline answered, "we came over to invite you to join our club. We thought, maybe, you'd like to?"

"My Land!" Jane stared from one to another of them. "And wear one of them blue-ribbon affairs?"

"Yes, indeed," Shirley laughed. "See, here it is," and she pointed to the one in Pauline's hand.

Sextoness Jane came down the steps. "Me, I ain't never wore a badge! Not once in all my life! Oncet, when I was a little youngster, 'most like Patience, teacher, she got up some sort of May doings. We was all to wear white dresses and red, white and blue ribbons—very night before, I come down with the mumps. Looks like I always come down when I ought to've stayed up!"

"But you won't come down with anything this time," Pauline pinned the blue badge on the waist of Jane's black and white calico. "Now you're an honorary member of 'The S. W. F. Club.'"

Jane passed a hand over it softly. "My Land!" was all she could say.

She was still stroking it softly as she walked slowly away towards home. My, wouldn't Tobias be interested!

CHAPTER IX

AT THE MANOR

" 'All the names I know from nurse:
    Gardener's garters, Shepherd's purse,
    Bachelor's buttons, Lady's smock,
    And the Lady Hollyhock,' "

Patience chanted, moving slowly about the parsonage garden, hands full of flowers, and the big basket, lying on the grass beyond, almost full.

Behind her, now running at full speed, now stopping suddenly, back lifted, tail erect, came Lucky, the black kitten from The Maples. Lucky had been an inmate of the parsonage for some weeks now and was thriving famously in her adopted home. Towser tolerated her with the indifference due such a small, insignificant creature, and she alternately bullied and patronized Towser.

"We haven't shepherd's purse, nor lady's

smock, that I know of, Lucky," Patience said, glancing back at the kitten, at that moment threatening battle at a polite nodding Sweet William, "but you can see for yourself that we have hollyhocks, while as for bachelor's buttons! Just look at that big, blue bunch in one corner of the basket."

It was the morning of the day of Shirley's turn and Pauline was hurrying to get ready to go over and help decorate the manor. She was singing, too; from the open windows of the "new room" came the words—

   " 'A cheerful world?—It surely is
     And if you understand your biz
     You'll taboo the worry worm,
     And cultivate the happy germ.' "

To which piece of good advice, Patience promptly whistled back the gay refrain.

On the back porch, Sextoness Jane—called in for an extra half-day—was ironing the white dresses to be worn that afternoon. And presently, Patience, her basket quite full and stowed away in the trap waiting before the side door, strolled around to interview her.

"I suppose you're going this afternoon?" she asked.

Jane looked up from waxing her iron. "Well, I was sort of calculating on going over for a bit; Miss Shirley having laid particular stress on my coming and this being the first reg'lar doings since I joined the club. I told her and Pauline they mustn't look for me to go junketing 'round with them all the while, seeing I'm in office—so to speak—and my time pretty well taken up with my work. I reckon you're going?"

"I—" Patience edged nearer the porch. Behind Jane stood the tall clothes-horse, with its burden of freshly ironed white things. At sight of a short, white frock, very crisp and immaculate, the blood rushed to the child's face, then as quickly receded.—After all, it would have had to be ironed for Sunday and —well, mother certainly had been very noncommittal the past few days—ever since that escapade with Bedelia, in fact—regarding her youngest daughter's hopes and fears for this all-important afternoon. And Patience had been wise enough not to press the matter.

"But, oh, I do wonder if Hilary has—" Patience went back to the side porch. Hilary was there talking to Bedelia. "You—you have fixed it up?" the child inquired anxiously.

Hilary looked gravely unconscious. "Fixed it up?" she repeated.

"About this afternoon—with mother?"

"Oh, yes! Mother's going; so is father."

Patience repressed a sudden desire to stamp her foot, and Hilary, seeing the real doubt and longing in her face, relented. "Mother wants to see you, Patty. I rather think there are to be conditions."

Patience darted off. From the doorway, she looked back—"I just knew you wouldn't go back on me, Hilary! I'll love you forever'n' ever."

Pauline came out a moment later, drawing on her driving gloves. "I feel like a storybook girl, going driving this time in the morning, in a trap like this. I wish you were coming, too, Hilary."

"Oh, I'm like the delicate story-book girl, who has to rest, so as to be ready for the dissipations that are to come later. I look the part, don't I?"

Pauline looked down into the laughing, sun-browned face. "If Uncle Paul were to see you now, he might find it hard to believe I hadn't—exaggerated that time."

"Well, it's your fault—and his, or was, in the beginning. You've a fine basket of flowers to take; Patience has done herself proud this morning."

"It's wonderful how well that young lady can behave—at times."

"Oh, she's young yet! When I hear mother tell how like her you used to be, I don't feel too discouraged about Patty."

"That strikes me as rather a double-edged sort of speech," Pauline gathered up the reins. "Good-by, and don't get too tired."

Shirley's turn was to be a combination studio tea and lawn-party, to which all club members, both regular and honorary, not to mention their relatives and friends, had been bidden. Following this, was to be a high tea for the regular members.

"That's Senior's share," Shirley had explained to Pauline. "He insists that it's up to him to do something."

Mr. Dayre was on very good terms with the "S. W. F. Club." As for Shirley, after the first, no one had ever thought of her as an outsider.

It was hard now, Pauline thought, as she drove briskly along, the lake breeze in her face, and the sound of Bedelia's quick trotting forming a pleasant accompaniment to her thoughts, very hard, to realize how soon the summer would be over. But perhaps—as Hilary said—next summer would mean the taking up again of this year's good times and interests,—Shirley talked of coming back. As for the winter—Pauline had in mind several plans for the winter. Those of the club members to stay behind must get together some day and talk them over. One thing was certain, the club motto must be lived up to bravely. If not in one way, why in another. There must be no slipping back into the old dreary rut and routine. It lay with themselves as to what their winter should be.

"And there's fine sleighing here, Bedelia,"

she said. "We'll get the old cutter out and give it a coat of paint."

Bedelia tossed her head, as if she heard in imagination the gay jingling of the sleigh-bells.

"But, in the meantime, here is the manor," Pauline laughed, "and it's the prettiest August day that ever was, and lawn-parties and such festivities are afoot, not sleighing parties."

The manor stood facing the lake with its back to the road, a broad sloping lawn surrounded it on three sides, with the garden at the back.

For so many seasons, it had stood lonely and neglected, that Pauline never came near it now, without rejoicing afresh in its altered aspect. Even the sight of Betsy Todd's dish towels, drying on the currant bushes at one side of the back door, added their touch to the sense of pleasant, homely life that seemed to envelop the old house nowadays.

Shirley came to the gate, as Pauline drew up, Phil, Pat and Pudgey in close attention. "I have to keep an eye on them," she told Pau-

line. "They've just had their baths, and
they're simply wild to get out in the middle
of the road and roll. I've told them no self-
respecting dog would wish to come to a lawn-
party in anything but the freshest of white
coats, but I'm afraid they're not very self-re-
specting."

"Patience is sure Towser's heart is heavy
because he is not to come; she has promised
him a lawn-party on his own account, and that
no grown-ups shall be invited. She's sent
you the promised flowers, and hinted—more
or less plainly—that she would have been
quite willing to deliver them in person."

"Why didn't you bring her? Oh, but I'm
afraid you've robbed yourself!"

"Oh, no, we haven't. Mother says, flowers
grow with picking."

"Come on around front," Shirley suggested. "The boys have been putting the
awning up."

"The boys" were three of Mr. Dayre's fellow artists, who had come up a day or two before, on a visit to the manor. One of them,
at any rate, deserved Shirley's title. He

came forward now. "Looks pretty nice, doesn't it?" he said, with a wave of the hand towards the red and white striped awning, placed at the further edge of the lawn.

Shirley smiled her approval, and introduced him to Pauline, adding that Miss Shaw was the real founder of their club.

"It's a might jolly sort of club, too," young Oram said.

"That is exactly what it has turned out to be," Pauline laughed. "Are the vases ready, Shirley?"

Shirley brought the tray of empty flower vases out on the veranda, and sent Harry Oram for a bucket of fresh water. "Harry is to make the salad," she explained to Pauline, as he came back. "Before he leaves the manor he will have developed into a fairly useful member of society."

"You've never eaten one of my salads, Miss Shaw," Harry said. "When you have, you'll think all your previous life an empty dream."

"It's much more likely her later life will prove a nightmare,—for a while, at least,"

Shirley declared. "Still, Paul, Harry does make them rather well. Betsy Todd, I am sorry to say, doesn't approve of him. But there are so many persons and things she doesn't approve of; lawn-parties among the latter."

Pauline nodded sympathetically; she knew Betsy Todd of old. Her wonder was, that the Dayres had been able to put up with her so long, and she said so.

" 'Hobson's choice,' " Shirley answered, with a little shrug. "She isn't much like our old Thèrese at home, is she, Harry? But nothing would tempt Thèrese away from her beloved New York. 'Vairmon! Nevaire have I heard of zat place!' she told Harry, when he interviewed her for us. Senior's gone to Vergennes—on business thoughts intent, or I hope they are. He's under strict orders not to 'discover a single bit' along the way, and to get back as quickly as possible."

"You see how beautifully she has us all in training?" Harry said to Pauline.

Pauline laughed. Suddenly she looked up from her flowers with sobered face. "I wonder," she said slowly, "if you know what it's meant to us—you're being here this summer, Shirley? Sometimes things do fit in just right after all. It's helped out wonderfully this summer, having you here and the manor open."

"Pauline has a fairy-story uncle down in New York," Shirley turned to Harry. "You've heard of him—Mr. Paul Shaw."

"Well,—rather! I've met him, once or twice—he didn't strike me as much of a believer in fairy tales."

"He's made us believe in them," Pauline answered.

"I think Senior might have provided me with such a delightful sort of uncle," Shirley observed. "I told him so, but he says, while he's awfully sorry I didn't mention it before, he's afraid it's too late now."

"Uncle Paul sent us Bedelia," Pauline told the rather perplexed-looking Harry, "and the row-boat and the camera and—oh, other things."

"Because he wanted them to have a nice, jolly summer," Shirley explained. "Pau-

line's sister had been sick and needed brightening up."

"You don't think he's looking around for
a nephew to adopt, do you?" Harry inquired. "A well-intentioned, intelligent
young man—with no end of talent."

"For making salads," Shirley added with a
sly smile.

"Oh, well, you know," Harry remarked
casually, "these are what Senior calls my
'salad days.'"

Whereupon Shirley rose without a word,
carrying off her vases of flowers.

The party at the manor was, like all the club
affairs, a decided success. Never had the old
place looked so gay and animated, since those
far-off days of its early glory.

The young people coming and going—the
girls in their light dresses and bright ribbons
made a pleasant place of the lawn, with its
background of shining water. The tennis
court, at one side of the house, was one of the
favorite gathering spots; there were one or
two boats out on the lake. The pleasant in-

formality of the whole affair proved its greatest charm.

Mr. Allen was there, pointing out to his host the supposed end of the subterranean passage said to connect the point on which the manor stood with the old ruined French fort over on the New York side. The minister was having a quiet chat with the doctor, who had made a special point of being there. Mothers of club members were exchanging notes and congratulating each other on the good comradeship and general air of contentment among the young people. Sextoness Jane was there, in all the glory of her best dress—one of Mrs. Shaw's handed-down summer ones—and with any amount of items picked up to carry home to Tobias, who was certain to expect a full account of this most unusual dissipation on his mistress's part. Even Betsy Todd condescended to put on her black woolen—usually reserved for church and funerals—and walk about among the other guests; but always, with an air that told plainly how little she approved of such goings on. The Boyds were there, their badges in full evidence. And last, though far from least, in her own estimation, Patience was there, very crisp and white and on her best behavior,—for, setting aside those conditions mother had seen fit to burden her with, was the delightful fact that Shirley had asked her to help serve tea.

The principal tea-table was in the studio, though there was a second one, presided over by Pauline and Bell, out under the awning at the edge of the lawn.

Patience thought the studio the very nicest room she had ever been in. It was long and low—in reality, the old dancing-hall, for the manor had been built after the pattern of its first owner's English home; and in the deep, recessed windows, facing the lake, many a be-patched and powdered little belle of Colonial days had coquetted across her fan with her bravely-clad partner.

Mr. Dayre had thrown out an extra window at one end, at right angles to the great stone fireplace, banked to-day with golden rod, thereby securing the desired north light.

On the easel, stood a nearly finished painting,—a sunny corner of the old manor kitchen, with Betsy Todd in lilac print gown, peeling apples by the open window, through which one caught a glimpse of the tall hollyhocks in the garden beyond.

Before this portrait, Patience found Sextoness Jane standing in mute astonishment.

"Betsy looks like she was just going to say —'take your hands out of the dish!' doesn't she?" Patience commented. Betsy had once helped out at the parsonage, during a brief illness of Miranda's, and the young lady knew whereof she spoke.

"I'd never've thought," Jane said slowly, "that anyone'd get that fond of Sister Todd —as to want a picture of her!"

"Oh, it's because she's such a character, you know," Patience explained serenely. Jane was so good about letting one explain things. "'A perfect character,' I heard one of those artist men say so."

Jane shook her head dubiously. "Not what I'd call a 'perfect' character—not that I've got anything against Sister Todd; but she's too fond of finding out a body's faults."

Patience went off then in search of empty tea-cups. She was having a beautiful time; at present only one cloud overshadowed her horizon. Already some tiresome folks were beginning to think about going. There was the talk of chores to be done, suppers to get, and with the breaking up, must come an end to her share in the party. For mother, though approached in the most delicate fashion, had proved obdurate regarding the further festivity to follow. Had mother been willing to consider the matter, Patience would have cheerfully undertaken to procure the necessary invitation. Shirley was a very obliging girl.

"And really, my dears," she said, addressing the three P's collectively, "it does seem a pity to have to go home before the fun's all over. And I could manage it—Bob would take me out rowing—if I coaxed—he rows very slowly. I don't suppose, for one moment, that we would get back in time. I believe—" For fully three minutes, Patience sat quite still in one of the studio window seats, oblivious of the chatter going on all about her; then into her blue eyes came a look not seen there very often—"No," she said sternly, shaking her head at Phil, much to his surprise, for he wasn't doing anything. "No —it wouldn't be *square*—and there would be the most awful to-do afterwards."

When a moment or two later, Mrs. Shaw called to her to come, that father was waiting, Patience responded with a very good grace. But Mr. Dayre caught the wistful look in the child's face. "Bless me," he said heartily. "You're not going to take Patience home with you, Mrs. Shaw? Let her stay for the tea—the young people won't keep late hours, I assure you."

"But I think—" Mrs. Shaw began very soberly.

"Sometimes, I find it quite as well not to think things over," Mr. Dayre suggested. "Why, dear me, I'd quite counted on Patience's being here. You see, I'm not a regular member, either; and I want someone to keep me in countenance."

So presently, Hilary felt a hand slipped eagerly into hers. "I'm staying! I'm staying!" an excited little voice announced. "And oh, I just love Mr. Dayre!"

Then Patience went back to her window seat to play the delightful game of "making believe" she hadn't stayed. She imagined that instead, she was sitting between father and mother in the gig, bubbling over with the desire to "hi-yi" at Fanny, picking her slow way along.

The studio was empty, even the dogs were outside, speeding the parting guests with more zeal than discretion. But after awhile Harry Oram strolled in.

"I'm staying!" Patience announced. She approved of Harry. "You're an artist, too, aren't you?" she remarked.

"So kind of you to say so," Harry murmured. "I have heard grave doubts expressed on the subject by my too impartial friends."

"I mean to be one when I grow up," Patience told him, "so's I can have a room like this—with just rugs on the floor; rugs slide so nicely—and window seats and things all cluttery."

"May I come and have tea with you? I'd like it awfully."

"It'll be really tea—not pretend kind," Patience said. "But I'll have that sort for any children who may come. Hilary takes pictures—she doesn't make them though. Made pictures are nicer, aren't they?"

"Some of them." Harry glanced through the open doorway, to where Hilary sat resting. She was "making" a picture now, he thought to himself, in her white dress, under the big tree, her pretty hair forming a frame about her thoughtful face. Taking a portfolio from a table near by, he went out to where Hilary sat.

"Your small sister says you take pictures," he said, drawing a chair up beside hers, "so I thought perhaps you'd let me show you these —they were taken by a friend of mine."

"Oh, but mine aren't anything like these! These are beautiful!" Hilary bent over the photographs he handed her; marveling over their soft tones. They were mostly bits of landscape, with here and there a water view and one or two fleecy cloud effects. It hardly seemed as though they could be really photographs.

"I've never done anything like these!" she said regretfully. "I wish I could—there are some beautiful views about here that would make charming pictures."

"She didn't in the beginning," Harry said. "She's lame; it was an accident, but she can never be quite well again, so she took this up, as an amusement at first, but now it's going to be her profession."

Hilary bent over the photographs again. "And you really think—anyone could learn to do it?"

"No, not anyone; but I don't see why the right sort of person couldn't."

"I wonder—if I could develop into the right sort."

"May I come and see what you have done —and talk it over?" Harry asked. "Since this friend of mine took it up, I'm ever so interested in camera work."

"Indeed you may," Hilary answered. She had never thought of her camera holding such possibilities within it, of it's growing into something better and more satisfying than a mere playmate of the moment.

"Rested?" Pauline asked, coming up. "Supper's nearly ready."

"I wasn't very tired. Paul, come and look at these."

Supper was served on the lawn; the pleasantest, most informal, of affairs, the presence of the older members of the party serving to turn the gay give and take of the young folks into deeper and wider channels, and Shirley's frequent though involuntary—"Do you remember, Senior?" calling out more than one vivid bit of travel, of description of places, known to most of them only through books.

Later, down on the lower end of the lawn, with the moon making a path of silver along the water, and the soft hush of the summer night over everything, Shirley brought out her guitar, singing for them strange folk-songs, picked up in her rambles with her father. Afterwards, the whole party sang songs that they all knew, ending up at last with the club song.

" 'It's a habit to be happy,' " the fresh

young voices chorused, sending the tune far
out across the lake; and presently, from a
boat on its further side, it was whistled back
to them.

"Who is it, I wonder?" Edna said.

"Give it up," Tom answered. "Someone who's heard it—there've been plenty of
opportunities for folks to hear it."

"Well it isn't a bad gospel to scatter broad-
cast," Bob remarked.

"And maybe it's someone who doesn't live
about here, and he will go away taking our
tune with him, for other people to catch up,"
Hilary suggested.

"But if he only has the tune and not the
words," Josie objected, "what use will that
be?"

"The spirit of the words is in the tune,"
Pauline said. "No one could whistle or sing
it and stay grumpy."

"They'd have to 'put the frown away
awhile, and try a little sunny smile,' wouldn't
they?" Patience observed.

Patience had been a model of behavior all
the evening. Mother would be sure to ask

if she had been good, when they got home.
That was one of those aggravating questions
that only time could relieve her from. No
one ever asked Paul, or Hilary, that—when
they'd been anywhere.

As Mr. Dayre had promised, the party
broke up early, going off in the various rigs
they had come in. Tom and Josie went in
the trap with the Shaws. "It's been perfectly
lovely—all of it," Josie said, looking back
along the road they were leaving. "Every
good time we have seems the best one yet."

"You wait 'til my turn comes," Pauline
told her. "I've such a scheme in my head."

"Am I in it?" Patience begged. She was
in front, between Tom, who was driving, and
Hilary, then she leaned forward, they were
nearly home, and the lights of the parsonage
showed through the trees. "There's a light
in the parlor—there's company!"

Pauline looked, too. "And one up in our
old room, Hilary. Goodness, it must be a
visiting minister! I didn't know father was
expecting anyone."

"I bet you!" Patience jumped excitedly up

and down. "I just bet it isn't any visiting
minister—but a visiting—uncle! I feel it in
my bones, as Miranda says."

"Nonsense!" Pauline declared.

"Maybe it isn't nonsense, Paul!" Hilary
said.

"I feel it in my bones," Patience repeated.
"I just *knew* Uncle Paul would come up—a
story-book uncle would be sure to."

"Well, here we are," Tom laughed.
"You'll know for certain pretty quick."

CHAPTER X

THE END OF SUMMER

IT was Uncle Paul, and perhaps no one was more surprised at his unexpected coming, than he himself.

That snap-shot of Hilary's had considerable to do with it; bringing home to him the sudden realization of the passing of the years. For the first time, he had allowed himself to face the fact that it was some time now since he had crossed the summit of the hill, and that under present conditions, his old age promised to be a lonely, cheerless affair.

He had never had much to do with young people; but, all at once, it seemed to him that it might prove worth his while to cultivate the closer acquaintance of these nieces of his. Pauline, in particular, struck him as likely to improve upon a nearer acquaintance. And that afternoon, as he rode up Broadway, he found himself wondering how she would enjoy the ride; and all the sights and wonders of the great city.

Later, over his solitary dinner, he suddenly decided to run up to Winton the next day. He would not wire them, he would rather like to take Phil by surprise.

So he had arrived at the parsonage, driving up in Jed's solitary hack, and much plied with information, general and personal, on the way, just as the minister and his wife reached home from the manor.

"And, oh, my! Doesn't father look tickled to death!" Patience declared, coming in to her sisters' room that night, ostensibly to have an obstinate knot untied, but inwardly determined to make a third at the usual bedtime talk for that once, at least. It wasn't often they all came up together.

"He looks mighty glad," Pauline said.

"And isn't it funny, hearing him called Phil?" Patience curled herself up in the cozy corner. "I never've thought of father as Phil."

Hilary paused in the braiding of her long

hair. "I'm glad we've got to know him—
Uncle Paul, I mean—through his letters, and
all the lovely things he's done for us; else, I
think I'd have been very much afraid of
him."

"So am I," Pauline assented. "I see now
what Mr. Oram meant—he doesn't look as if
he believed much in fairy stories. But I like
his looks—he's so nice and tall and straight."

"He used to have red hair, before it turned
gray," Hilary said, "so that must be a family
trait; your chin's like his, Paul, too,—so
square and determined."

"Is mine?" Patience demanded.

"You cut to bed, youngster," Pauline commanded. "You're losing all your beauty
sleep; and really, you know—"

Patience went to stand before the mirror.
"Maybe I ain't—pretty—yet; but I'm going
to be—some day. Mr. Dayre says he likes
red hair, I asked him. He says for me not to
worry; I'll have them all sitting up and taking notice yet."

At which Pauline bore promptly down
upon her, escorting her in person to the door

of her own room. "And you'd better get to bed pretty quickly, too, Hilary," she advised, coming back. "You've had enough excitement for one day."

Mr. Paul Shaw stayed a week; it was a busy week for the parsonage folk and for some other people besides. Before it was over, the story-book uncle had come to know his nieces and Winton fairly thoroughly; while they, on their side, had grown very well acquainted with the tall, rather silent man, who had a fashion of suggesting the most delightful things to do in the most matter-of-fact manner.

There were one or two trips decidedly outside that ten-mile limit, including an all day sail up the lake, stopping for the night at a hotel on the New York shore and returning by the next day's boat. There was a visit to Vergennes, which took in a round of the shops, a concert, and another night away from home.

"Was there ever such a week!" Hilary sighed blissfully one morning, as she and her uncle waited on the porch for Bedelia and the trap. Hilary was to drive him over to The Maples for dinner.

"Or such a summer altogether," Pauline added, from just inside the study window.

"Then Winton has possibilities?" Mr. Shaw asked.

"I should think it has; we ought to be eternally grateful to you for making us find them out," Pauline declared.

Mr. Shaw smiled, more as if to himself. "I daresay they're not all exhausted yet."

"Perhaps," Hilary said slowly, "some places are like some people, the longer and better you know them, the more you keep finding out in them to like."

"Father says," Pauline suggested, "that one finds, as a rule, what one is looking for."

"Here we are," her uncle exclaimed, as Patience appeared, driving Bedelia. "Do you know," he said, as he and Hilary turned out into the wide village street, "I haven't seen the schoolhouse yet?"

"We can go around that way. It isn't much of a building," Hilary answered.

"I suppose it serves its purpose."

"It is said to be a very good school for the size of the place." Hilary turned Bedelia up the little by-road, leading to the old weather-beaten schoolhouse, standing back from the road in an open space of bare ground.

"You and Pauline are through here?" her uncle asked.

"Paul is. I would've been this June, if I hadn't broken down last winter."

"You will be able to go on this fall?"

"Yes, indeed. Dr. Brice said so the other day. He says, if all his patients got on so well, by not following his advice, he'd have to shut up shop, but that, fortunately for him, they haven't all got a wise uncle down in New York, to offer counter-advice."

"Each in his turn," Mr. Shaw remarked, adding, "and Pauline considers herself through school?"

"I—I suppose so. I know she would like to go on—but we've no higher school here and —She read last winter, quite a little, with father. Pauline's ever so clever."

"Supposing you both had an opportunity—

for it must be both, or neither, I judge—and the powers that be consented—how about going away to school this winter?"

Hilary dropped the reins. "Oh!" she cried, "you mean—"

"I have a trick of meaning what I say," her uncle said, smiling at her.

"I wish I could say—what I want to—and can't find words for—" Hilary said.

"We haven't consulted the higher authorities yet, you know."

"And—Oh, I don't see how mother could get on without us, even if—"

"Mothers have a knack at getting along without a good many things—when it means helping their young folks on a bit," Mr. Shaw remarked. "I'll have a talk with her and your father to-night."

That evening, pacing up and down the front veranda with his brother, Mr. Shaw said, with his customary abruptness, "You seem to have fitted in here, Phil,—perhaps, you were in the right of it, after all. I take it you haven't had such a hard time, in some ways."

The minister did not answer immediately. Looking back nearly twenty years, he told himself, that he did not regret that early choice of his. He had fitted into the life here; he and his people had grown together. It had not always been smooth sailing and more than once, especially the past year or so, his narrow means had pressed him sorely, but on the whole, he had found his lines cast in a pleasant place, and was not disposed to rebel against his heritage.

"Yes," he said, at last, "I have fitted in; too easily, perhaps. I never was ambitious, you know."

"Except in the accumulating of books," his brother suggested.

The minister smiled. "I have not been able to give unlimited rein even to that mild ambition. Fortunately, the rarer the opportunity, the greater the pleasure it brings with it—and the old books never lose their charm."

Mr. Paul Shaw flicked the ashes from his cigar. "And the girls—you expect them to fit in, too?"

"It is their home." A note the elder brother knew of old sounded in the younger man's voice.

"Don't mount your high horse just yet, Phil," he said. "I'm not going to rub you up the wrong way—at least, I don't mean to; but you were always an uncommonly hard chap to handle—in some matters. I grant you, it is their home and not a bad sort of home for a girl to grow up in." Mr. Shaw stood for a moment at the head of the steps, looking off down the peaceful, shadowy street. It had been a pleasant week; he had enjoyed it wonderfully. He meant to have many more such. But to live here always! Already the city was calling to him; he was homesick for its rush and bustle, the sense of life and movement.

"You and I stand as far apart to-day, in some matters, Phil, as we did twenty—thirty years ago," he said presently, "and that eldest daughter of yours—I'm a fair hand at reading character or I shouldn't be where I am to-day, if I were not—is more like me than you."

"So I have come to think—lately."

"That second girl takes after you; she would never have written that letter to me last May."

"No, Hilary would not have at the time—"

"Oh, I can guess how you felt about it at the time. But, look here, Phil, you've got over that—surely? After all, I like to think now that Pauline only hurried on the inevitable." Mr. Paul Shaw laid his hand on the minister's shoulder. "Nearly twenty years is a pretty big piece out of a lifetime. I see now how much I have been losing all these years."

"It has been a long time, Paul; and, perhaps, I have been to blame in not trying more persistently to heal the breach between us. I assure you that I have regretted it daily."

"You always did have a lot more pride in your make-up than a man of your profession has any right to allow himself, Phil. But if you like, I'm prepared to point out to you right now how you can make it up to me. Here comes Lady Shaw and we won't waste time getting to business."

That night, as Pauline and Hilary were in their own room, busily discussing, for by no

means the first time that day, what Uncle Paul
had said to Hilary that morning, and just
how he had looked, when he said it, and was
it at all possible that father would consent,
and so on, *ad libitum,* their mother tapped at
the door.

Pauline ran to open it. "Good news, or
not?" she demanded. "Yes, or no, Mother
Shaw?"

"That is how you take it," Mrs. Shaw answered. She was glad, very glad, that this
unforeseen opportunity should be given her
daughters; and yet—it meant the first break
in the home circle, the first leaving home for
them.

Mr. Paul Shaw left the next morning.
"I'll try and run up for a day or two, before
the girls go to school," he promised his sister-
in-law. "Let me know, as soon as you have
decided *where* to send them."

Patience was divided in her opinion, as to
this new plan. It would be lonesome without
Paul and Hilary; but then, for the time being, she would be, to all intents and purposes,

"Miss Shaw." Also, Bedelia was not going to boarding-school—on the whole, the arrangement had its advantages. Of course, later, she would have her turn at school—Patience meant to devote a good deal of her winter's reading to boarding-school stories.

She told Sextoness Jane so, when that person appeared, just before supper time.

Jane looked impressed. "A lot of things keep happening to you folks right along," she observed. "Nothing's ever happened to me, 'cept mumps—and things of that sort; you wouldn't call them interesting. The girls to home?"

"They're 'round on the porch, looking at some photos Mr. Oram's brought over; and he's looking at Hilary's. Hilary's going in for some other kind of picture taking. I wish she'd leave her camera home, when she goes to school. Do you want to speak to them about anything particular?"

"I'll wait a bit," Jane sat down on the garden-bench beside Patience.

"There, he's gone!" the latter said, as the front gate clicked a few moments later. "O

Paul!" she called, "You're wanted, Paul!"

"You and Hilary going to be busy to-night?" Jane asked, as Pauline came across the lawn.

"Not that I know of."

"I ain't," Patience remarked.

"Well," Jane said, "it ain't prayer-meeting night, and it ain't young peoples' night and it ain't choir practice night, so I thought maybe you'd like me to take my turn at showing you something. Not all the club—like's not they wouldn't care for it, but if you think they would, why, you can show it to them some-time."

"Just we three then?" Pauline asked. "Hilary and I can go."

"So can I—if you tell mother you want me to," Patience put in.

"Is it far?" her sister questioned Jane.

"A good two miles—we'd best walk—we can rest after we get there. Maybe, if you like, you'd better ask Tom and Josie. Your ma'll be better satisfied if he goes along, I reckon. I'll come for you at about half-past seven."

"All right, thank you ever so much," Pauline said, and went to tell Hilary, closely pursued by Patience. However, Mrs. Shaw vetoed Pauline's proposition that Patience should make one of the party.

"Not every time, my dear," she explained.

Promptly at half-past seven Jane appeared. "All ready?" she said, as the four young people came to meet her. "You don't want to go expecting anything out of the common. Like's not, you've all seen it a heap of times, but maybe not to take particular notice of it."

She led the way through the garden to the lane running past her cottage, where Tobias sat in solitary dignity on the doorstep, down the lane to where it merged in to what was nothing more than a field path.

"Are we going to the lake?" Hilary asked.

Jane nodded.

"But not out on the water," Josie said. "You're taking us too far below the pier for that."

Jane smiled quietly. "It'll be *on* the water —what you're going to see," she was getting a good deal of pleasure out of her small mystery, and when they reached the low shore, fringed with the tall sea-grass, she took her party a few steps along it to where an old log lay a little back from the water. "I reckon we'll have to wait a bit," she said, "but it'll be 'long directly."

They sat down in a row, the young people rather mystified. Apparently the broad expanse of almost motionless water was quite deserted. There was a light breeze blowing and the soft swishing of the tiny waves against the bank was the only sound to break the stillness; the sky above the long irregular range of mountains on the New York side, still wore its sunset colors, the lake below sending back a faint reflection of them.

But presently these faded until only the afterglow was left, to merge in turn into the soft summer twilight, through which the stars began to glimpse, one by one.

The little group had been mostly silent, each busy with his or her thoughts; so far as the young people were concerned, happy thoughts enough; for if the closing of each day brought their summer nearer to its ending, the fall would bring with it new experiences, an entering of new scenes.

"There!" Sextoness Jane broke the silence, pointing up the lake, to where a tiny point of red showed like a low-hung star through the gathering darkness. Moment by moment, other lights came into view, silently, steadily, until it seemed like some long, gliding sea-serpent, creeping down towards them through the night.

"A tow!" Josie cried under her breath.

They had all seen it, times without number, before. The long line of canal boats being towed down the lake to the canal below; the red lanterns at either end of each boat showing as they came. But to-night, infected perhaps, by the pride, the evident delight, in Jane's voice, the old familiar sight held them with the new interest the past months had brought to bear upon so many old, familiar things.

"It is—wonderful," Pauline said at last. "It might be a scene from—fairyland, almost."

"Me—I love to see them come stealing long like that through the dark," Jane said slowly and a little hesitatingly. It was odd to be telling confidences to anyone except Tobias. "I don't know where they come from, nor where they're a-going to. Many's the night I walk over here just on the chance of seeing one. Mostly, this time of year, you're pretty likely to catch one. When I was younger, I used to sit and fancy myself going aboard on one of them and setting off for strange parts. I wasn't looking to settle down here in Winton all my days; but I reckon, maybe, it's just's well—anyhow, when I got the freedom to travel, I'd got out of the notion of it—and perhaps, there's no telling, I might have been terribly disappointed. And there ain't any hindrance 'gainst my setting off—in my own mind—every time I sits here and watches a tow go down the lake. I've seen a heap of big churches in my travels—it's mostly easier 'magining about them—churches are pretty much alike I reckon, though I ain't seen many, I'll admit."

No one answered for a moment, but Jane,

used to Tobias for a listener, did not mind.
Then in the darkness, Hilary laid a hand
softly over the work-worn ones clasped on
Jane's lap. It was hard to imagine Jane
young and full of youthful fancies and longings; yet years ago there had been a Jane—
not Sextoness Jane then—who had found
Winton dull and dreary and had longed to get
away. But for her, there had been no one to
wave the magic wand, that should transform
the little Vermont village into a place filled
with new and unexplored charms. Never in
all Jane's many summers, had she known one
like this summer of theirs; and for them—the
wonder was by no means over—the years
ahead were bright with untold possibilities.
Hilary sighed for very happiness, wondering
if she were the same girl who had rocked listlessly in the hammock that June morning,
protesting that she didn't care for "half-way"
things.

"Tired?" Pauline asked.

"I was thinking," her sister answered.

"Well, the tow's gone." Jane got up to
go.

"I'm ever so glad we came, thank you so much, Jane," Pauline said heartily.

"I wonder what'll have happened by the time we all see our next tow go down," Josie said, as they started towards home.

"We may see a good many more than one before the general exodus," her brother answered.

"But we won't have time to come watch for them. Oh, Paul, just think, only a little while now—"

Tom slipped into step with Hilary, a little behind the others. "I never supposed the old soul had it in her," he said, glancing to where Jane trudged heavily on ahead. "Still, I suppose she was young—once; though I've never thought of her being so before."

"Yes," Hilary said. "I wonder,—maybe, she's been better off, after all, right here at home. She wouldn't have got to be Sextoness Jane anywhere else, probably."

Tom glanced at her quickly. "Is there a hidden meaning—subject to be carefully avoided?"

Hilary laughed. "As you like."

"So you and Paul are off on your travels, too?"

"Yes, though I can hardly believe it yet."

"And just as glad to go as any of us."

"Oh, but we're coming back—after we've been taught all manner of necessary things."

"Edna'll be the only one of you girls left behind; it's rough on her."

"It certainly is; we'll all have to write her heaps of letters."

"Much time there'll be for letter-writing, outside of the home ones," Tom said.

"Speaking of time," Josie turned towards them, "we're going to be busier than any bee ever dreamed of being, before or since Dr. Watts."

They certainly were busy days that followed. So many of the young folks were going off that fall that a good many of the meetings of "The S. W. F. Club" resolved themselves into sewing-bees, for the girl members only.

"If we'd known how jolly they were, we'd have tried them before," Bell declared one morning, dropping down on the rug Pauline had spread under the trees at one end of the parsonage lawn.

Patience, pulling bastings with a business-like air, nodded her curly head wisely. "Miranda says, folks mostly get 'round to enjoying their blessings 'bout the time they come to lose them."

"Has the all-important question been settled yet, Paul?" Edna asked, looking up from her work. She might not be going away to school, but even so, that did not debar one from new fall clothes at home.

"They're coming to Vergennes with me," Bell said. "Then we can all come home together Friday nights."

"They're coming to Boston with me," Josie corrected, "then we'll be back together for Thanksgiving."

Shirley, meekly taking her first sewing lessons under Pauline's instructions, and frankly declaring that she didn't at all like them, dropped the hem she was turning. "They're coming to New York with me; and in the between-times we'll have such fun that they'll never want to come home."

Pauline laughed. "It looks as though Hilary and I would have a busy winter between you all. It is a comfort to know where we are going."

"Remember!" she warned, when later the party broke up. "Four o'clock Friday afternoon! Sharp!"

"Are we going out in a blaze of glory?" Bell questioned.

"You might tell us where we are going, now, Paul?" Josie urged.

Pauline shook her head. "You wait until Friday, like good little girls. Mind, you all bring wraps; it'll be chilly coming home."

Pauline's turn was to be the final wind-up of the club's regular outings. No one outside the home folks, excepting Tom, had been taken into her confidence—it had been necessary to press him into service. And when, on Friday afternoon, the young people gathered at the parsonage, all but those named were still in the dark.

Besides the regular members, Mrs. Shaw, Mr. Dayre, Mr. Allen, Harry Oram and Patience were there; the minister and Dr. Brice had promised to join the party later if possible.

As a rule, the club picnics were coöperative affairs; but to-day the members, by special request, arrived empty-handed. Mr. Paul Shaw, learning that Pauline's turn was yet to come, had insisted on having a share in it.

"I am greatly interested in this club," he had explained. "I like results, and I think," he glanced at Hilary's bright happy face, "that the 'S. W. F. Club' has achieved at least one very good result."

And on the morning before the eventful Friday, a hamper had arrived from New York, the watching of the unpacking of which had again transformed Patience, for the time, from an interrogation to an exclamation point.

"It's a beautiful hamper," she explained to Towser. "It truly is—because father says, it's the inner, not the outer, self that makes for real beauty, or ugliness; and it certainly was the inside of that hamper that counted. I wish you were going, Towser. See here, suppose you follow on kind of quietly to-morrow afternoon—don't show up too soon, and I guess I can manage it."

Which piece of advice Towser must have understood. At any rate, he acted upon it to the best of his ability, following the party at a discreet distance through the garden and down the road towards the lake; and only when the halt at the pier came, did he venture near, the most insinuating of dogs.

And so successfully did Patience manage it, that when the last boat-load pushed off from shore, Towser sat erect on the narrow bow seat, blandly surveying his fellow voyagers. "He does so love picnics," Patience explained to Mr. Dayre, "and this is the last particular one for the season. I kind of thought he'd go along and I slipped in a little paper of bones."

From the boat ahead came the chorus. "We're out on the wide ocean sailing."

"Not much!" Bob declared. "I wish we were—the water's quiet as a mill-pond this afternoon."

For the great lake, appreciating perhaps the importance of the occasion, had of its many moods chosen to wear this afternoon its sweetest, most beguiling one, and lay, a broad stretch of sparkling, rippling water, between its curving shores.

Beyond, the range of mountains rose dark and somber against the cloud-flecked sky, their tops softened by the light haze that told of coming autumn.

And presently, from boat to boat, went the call, "We're going to Fort Edward! Why didn't we guess?"

"But that's not *in* Winton," Edna protested.

"Of it, if not in it," Jack Ward assured them.

"Do you reckon you can show us anything new about that old fort, Paul Shaw?" Tracy demanded. "Why, I could go all over it blindfolded."

"Not to show the new—to unfold the old," Pauline told him.

"That sounds like a quotation."

"It is—in substance," Pauline looked across her shoulder to where Mr. Allen sat, imparting information to Harry Oram.

"So that's why you asked the old fellow," Tracy said. "Was that kind?"

They were rounding the slender point on which the tall, white lighthouse stood, and entering the little cove where visitors to the fort usually beached their boats.

A few rods farther inland, rose the tall, grass-covered, circular embankment, surrounding the crumbling, gray walls, the outer shells of the old barracks.

At the entrance to the enclosure, Tom suddenly stepped ahead, barring the way. "No passing within this fort without the countersign," he declared. "Martial law, this afternoon."

It was Bell who discovered it. "'It's a habit to be happy,'" she suggested, and Tom drew back for her to enter. But one by one, he exacted the password from each.

Inside, within the shade of those old, gray walls, a camp-fire had been built and camp-kettle swung, hammocks had been hung under the trees and when cushions were scattered here and there the one-time fort bore anything but a martial air.

But something of the spirit of the past must have been in the air that afternoon, or perhaps, the spirit of the coming changes; for this picnic—though by no means lacking in charm—was not as gay and filled with light-hearted chaff as usual. There was more talking in quiet groups, or really serious searching for some trace of those long-ago days of storm and stress.

With the coming of evening, the fire was lighted and the cloth laid within range of its flickering shadows. The night breeze had sprung up and from outside the sloping embankment they caught the sound of the waves breaking on the beach. True to their promise, the minister and Dr. Brice appeared at the time appointed and were eagerly welcomed by the young people.

Supper was a long, delightful affair that night, with much talk of the days when the fort had been devoted to far other purposes than the present; and the young people, listening to the tales Mr. Allen told in his quiet yet strangely vivid way, seemed to hear the slow creeping on of the boats outside and to be listening in the pauses of the wind for the approach of the enemy.

"I'll take it back, Paul," Tracy told her, as they were repacking the baskets. "Even the old fort has developed new interests."

"And next summer the 'S. W. F. Club' will continue its good work," Jack said.

Going back, Pauline found herself sitting in the stern of one of the boats, beside her father. The club members were singing the club song. But Pauline's thoughts had suddenly gone back to that wet May afternoon.

She could see the dreary, rain-swept garden, hear the beating of the drops on the window-panes. How long ago and remote it all seemed; how far from the hopeless discontent, the vague longings, the real anxiety of that time, she and Hilary had traveled. She looked up impulsively. "There's one thing," she said, "we've had one summer that I shall always feel would be worth reliving. And we're going to have more of them."

"I am glad to hear that," Mr. Shaw said.

Pauline looked about her—the lanterns at the ends of the boats threw dancing lights out across the water, no longer quiet; overhead, the sky was bright with stars. "Everything is so beautiful," the girl said slowly. "One seems to feel it more—every day."

" 'The hearing ear, and the seeing eye, the Lord hath made even both of them,' " her father quoted gravely.

Pauline drew a quick breath. "The hearing ear and the seeing eye"—it was a good thought to take with them—out into the new life, among the new scenes. One would need them everywhere—out in the world, as well as in Winton. And then, from the boat just ahead, sounded Patience's clear treble,— " 'There's a Good Time Coming.' "